NATURE'S WONDERS

NATURE'S WONDERS

FOR THE YOUNG AT ART™

Creative Activities for Ages Six and Up
Using the Please Touch™ Philosophy

SUSAN STRIKER

Illustrations by Sally Schaedler

Maryann Craven and Emma Oberheuser
MUSIC CONSULTANTS

An Owl Book
Henry Holt and Company   New York

Henry Holt and Company, Inc.
Publishers since 1866
115 West 18th Street
New York, New York 10011

Henry Holt ® is a registered
trademark of Henry Holt and Company, Inc.

Published in Canada by Fitzhenry & Whiteside Ltd.,
195 Allstate Parkway, Markham, Ontario L3R 4T8.

Library of Congress Cataloging-in-Publication Data
Striker, Susan.
Nature's wonders for the young at art
using the please touch™ philosophy/Susan Striker;
illustrations by Sally Schaedler; music consultants,
Maryann Craven and Emma Oberheuser.—1st ed.
p.   cm.
"An owl book."
ISBN 0-8050-4806-5 (pbk.: alk. paper)
1. Art—Study and teaching (primary)—Activity programs.
2. Nature study—Activity programs. 3. Creative ability in children.
4. Perception in children. I. Schaedler, Sally. II. Title.
N361.S76 1999
372.5'044—dc21   98-34728

Henry Holt books are available for special
promotions and premiums. For details contact:
Director, Special Markets.

First Edition 1998

Printed in the United States of America
All first editions are printed on acid-free paper. ∞

1 3 5 7 9 10 8 6 4 2

Thanks to Annette Griffith and Carol Sarabun

for new beginnings and spring in Greenwich

Painters understand nature

and love her and

teach us to see her.

—VINCENT VAN GOGH

CONTENTS

ACKNOWLEDGMENTS

The music was chosen or specially written by my two dearest friends, music teachers Maryann Craven and Emma Oberheuser.

Thank you to Emma Oberheuser for typesetting the music so creatively and Diana Crofton, typist extraordinaire!

Thanks to Tim Marino, Joy Noble, Rhodie Rudolph, Margo Bittenbender, Maureen Rogers, Olive Sabato, Vinnie LaCour, and Mark Clark (aged 10) for being so generous with their talent and expertise.

A special thanks to Heidi Fong for translating "new beginnings" into Chinese calligraphy so beautifully.

INTRODUCTION

Like the flowers, trees, birds, animals, and insects we share the earth with, we are all a part of nature. What distinguishes us from the rest is our primal instinct to create. From the time of the earliest known cave dwellers, all civilizations have made art, composed music, and told stories. These arts have flourished in good times as well as bad. Our human instinct to create is so strong that it perseveres despite wars and famine. Children in concentration camps in Germany drew pictures, painfully similar to the pictures our own children make in school today.

We have used art to interpret nature and understand our place in it. Although there is absolutely nothing in nature that requires the use of a ruler to draw, "I can't draw a straight line with a ruler" has become the mantra of several generations. We continue to fight our own human nature to try to overcome it when we should be exploring it and finding our own rhythm and our own place in nature. From observing a tree we can learn so much: how important it is to put down deep roots, why we need to grow and flourish where we are planted, why we have to branch out, how to be flexible and bend when winds are harsh and strong. As the seasons of our lives change, our colors change, but they are still our true colors. They are equally rich and beautiful.

We need to learn how to appreciate all the seasons of our lives, how not to yearn for impending adulthood or lost youth. We need to live in harmony with nature and our own humanity. And we must remember what every civilization has known before us: creativity is fundamental to our humanity.

Art is the universal visual language. Children are not born knowing how to draw or paint any more than they are born knowing how to walk or talk. Talking begins with simple sounds, progresses to single words, then to groups of words, sentences, and eventually to the mastery of a language. In just the same way, art skills begin with scribbling and manipulation of materials, and moves through predictable stages of development until mastery is achieved. Yet, too often, although we are overjoyed by the first *mama* and recognize it as the first step on a long road to fluency and we clap and cheer when our children take their first tentative, clumsy steps, we ignore their first scribbles or, worse still, express only disappointment when their artistic impulses are found scribbled on inappropriate surfaces.

We all have a basic need to express ourselves through art and a natural instinct for esthetics. People who look at great abstract art and say "my four-year-old can do that!" are in touch with an important truth. Implicit in that statement, however, is the sad fact that by age twenty-one, very few of us still rely on our natural instincts for good design or have confidence in our creative impulses.

What happens in the interim? Too often, parents and teachers, who themselves feel inadequate in art, give children pat formulas for drawing and adult-created pictures to trace, color in, and copy. These activities serve no purpose but to perpetuate a sense of inadequacy and squelch the quest for discovery. Even talented and creative art teachers can do a great disservice to their students when they involve them in ever-changing art activities. What children really need in order to become literate in art is a combination of two essential ingredients in each project they attempt:

1. A chance to freely create and express them selves without caring about right or wrong.

2. A sequential, step-by-step exploration of materials, skills, and concepts that will aid them in attaining their own goals.

At the end of *Nature's Wonders* I have included a list of *concepts* that I developed over many years of teaching art. I use them as my goals when preparing art activities for my students and readers. I also include the relevant National Standards that they address.

Teaching art does not involve showing someone how to draw a particular thing. It involves offering the child opportunities to learn the fundamental skills. It enables the child to make whatever he or she wants to make. It also involves giving a child the confidence, skills, and enthusiasm to carry out any art activity in a manner that is appropriate to his or her age and interest. I have used storytelling and music to motivate children to create art, and in this book I share some of these ways to maximize the impact of an art experience. The inspiration to create art is an integral part of the creative process. As my students congregate in the "reading corner" of my art room before each class, we enjoy a story together that serves as an important introduction to an art activity. We know: "In the beginning, there was the word."

Each section of *Nature's Wonders* contains at least one out-of-book activity, as well as space to draw in the book itself. Related music and stories are recommended. There is no wrong way for the young at art to explore or express their creativity.

NATURE'S
WONDERS

ANIMAL ACTIVITIES

MATERIALS

- 3″ × 5″ (or other "hand size") paper bag
- 9″ × 6″ cardboard
- 9″ × 6″ colored construction paper
- Black paper scraps
- Fluorescent (or other brightly colored) paper scraps
- Newspaper
- Rubber bands
- Pencils
- Optional: Yarn or raffia

CONCEPTS

Using your imagination

Three-dimensional art

TO READ

Monsters by Russell Hoban

LISTEN TO

"In the Hall of the Mountain King" from the *Peer Gynt Suite* by Edvard Grieg

INSTRUCTIONS

1. Paste 9″ × 6″ colored paper to 9″ × 6″ cardboard. Turn it over.
2. Draw two connected feet to support monster. Cut out feet.
3. Add details, such as toenails or shoes.
4. Crumple newspaper and fill paper bag with it.
5. Secure top of bag with a rubber band.

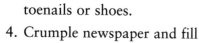

6. Cut out eyes, ears, nose, horns, etc., from fluorescent paper.
7. Paste each feature on black paper and cut around it so that each brightly colored detail is framed in black to provide color contrast.
8. Paste features on monster.
9. Use curled paper, yarn, or raffia for hair, beard, etc.

TO SING

Monsters All Around

Marianne Craven

There's mon-sters all a-round us   ma-ny to be found

some live in the o—cean   some walk on the ground   If you go to Scotland——

I've heard it is said,   A mon-ster lives in the Lock Ness   ma-ny have seen its head.

There's monsters all around us, etc.

In the Himalayas
Way up in the sky
There lives a Yeti Monster
He stands eight feet high.

There's monsters all around us, etc.

So do be very careful
When you travel 'round—
A monster may be near you
You may not hear a sound.

There's monsters all around us, etc.

2

Monster Sighted!

The Loch Ness Monster lives in Scotland, the Abominable Snowman lives in the Himalayas. What if a monster was discovered in your town?

Illustrations by Sally Schaedler © Susan Striker

3

Who Built the Ark?

American Folk Song
Arranged by Bruce Simpson

Refrain

Who built the ark? No - ah, No - ah, Who built the ark? Brother Noah built the ark.

Fine

Verse

1. Now didn't old No - ah build the ark?
   built it long, both wide and tall,
   in come the an - i - mals two by two,
   in come the an - i - mals three by three,

He built it out of a hick-o-ry bark,
Plenty of room for the large and small,
Hip - po - pota - mus and kan - ga - roo,
Two big cats and a bum - ble bee.

2.He
3.Now
4.Now

After each four verses D.C.

MATERIALS

Pariscraft™

Warm water

Newspaper

Masking tape

Scissors

Wiggly eyes

Glue

Pencils

TO SING

5. Now in come the animals four by four,
   Two through the window and two through the door.
6. Now in come the animals five by five,
   Four little sparrows and the redbird's wife.
7. Now in come the animals six by six,
   Elephant laughed at the monkey's tricks.
8. Now in come the animals seven by seven,
   Four from home and the rest from heaven.
9. Now in come the animals eight by eight,
   Some were on time and the others were late.
10. Now in come the animals nine by nine,
    Some was a-shouting and some was a-crying.
11. Now in come the animals ten by ten,
    Five black roosters and five black hens.
12. Now Noah says, "Go shut that door,
    The rain's started dropping and we can't take more."

TO READ

Barnyard Banter by Denise Fleming

Noah's Ark retold by Lucy Cousins

A Twist in the Tail: Animal Stories from Around the World
by Mary Hoffman and Jan Ormerod

Illustrations by Sally Schaedler © Susan Striker

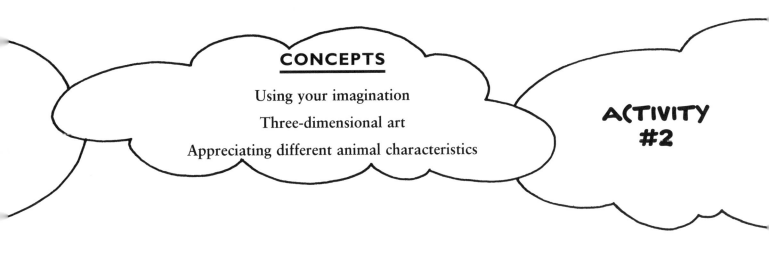

INSTRUCTIONS

1. To create a rare animal of your own, crumple newspaper into the shape of an animal.

2. Secure with masking tape.

3. Cut Pariscraft into Band-Aid sized strips.

4. Dip each piece into warm water and count to 10.

5. Cover animal with overlapping strips, smoothing out wrinkles as you go along.

6. Allow to dry.

7. Paint and allow to dry.

8. Add details, such as wiggly eyes, tail, etc.

What would the ark look like if it were built in modern times?

Illustrations by Sally Schaedler © Susan Striker

ACTIVITY #3

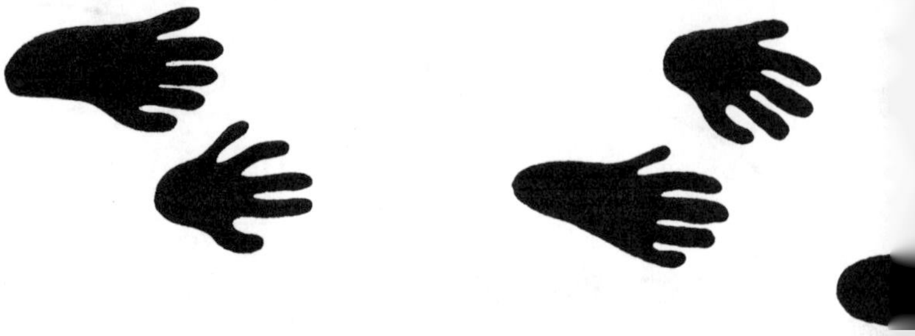

TO READ

Wipe Your Feet!
by Daniel Lehan

Whose Footprints?
by Molly Coxe

Watch William Walk
by Ann Jonas

Animal Tracks of Alaska
by Chris Stall

MATERIALS

 Erasers

 X-Acto knife

 Tempera paint

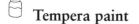 Paper

INSTRUCTIONS

1. Read the book
Wipe Your Feet! or *Whose Footprints?*
2. Carve an eraser for each creature's footprint and print across the paper.

"These Footprints I am Making"

These footprints I am making

Know that I am real,

that I have real feet

that I am big enough

to matter.

And they will show whoever

happens by

that I was here FIRST.

—from *A Moon in Your Lunch Box*
by Michael Spooner

dog

CONCEPTS

Printing

Pattern

cottontail rabbit

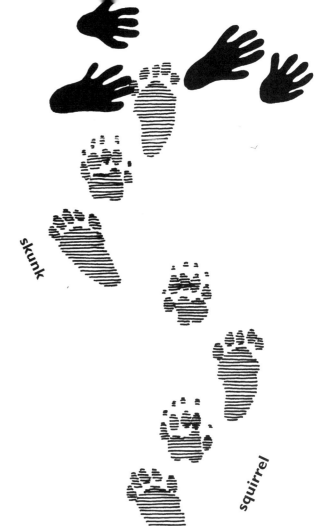

skunk

squirrel

opossum

Footprints create patterns in the sand to tell us stories, if we can read them. Can you tell a story, just by drawing footprints?

raccoon

deer

Illustrations by Sally Schaedler © Susan Striker

CONCEPTS

Using soft drawing utensils

Multicultural awareness

Increasing perception of the world around us

MATERIALS

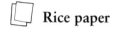 Rice paper   Charcoal

Wood strips   Staple gun and staples

Hinges   Screwdriver and screws

TO READ

The Boy Who Drew Cats by Archer A. Levine

Cat and Rat by Ed Young

Spooky Night by Natalie Savage Carlson

Cats (Looking at Paintings) by Peggy Roalf

INSTRUCTIONS

1. Read one of the books suggested.
2. To build a screen: using a staple gun, attach wooden strips together to create frames.
3. Stretch rice paper over wooden strips and staple.
4. Connect screen panels with hinges.
5. With charcoal, draw cats on one panel while your friends draw cats on other panels.

TO SING

The Cat Came Back

traditional american folk
arr. Joan Fretz c 1991

1. Once there was man who had troubles of his own. He had a yel-low cat which wouldn't leav it's home. He tried and he tried to give the cat away. He gave it to a man go-ing far a way. But the

Chorus

cat came back the ve-ry next day. The cat came back, they thought he was a gon- er, but the cat came back, he just couldn't stay a - way.

2.(He)

2. He gave it to a man going way out west;
   Told him to take it to the one he loved the best.
   The train hit the curve and then it jumped the rail;
   Not a soul was left behind to tell the gruesome tale.

CHORUS

3. The man around the corner swore he'd shoot the cat on sight;
   He loaded up his shotgun with nails and dynamite.
   He waited and he waited for the cat to come around;
   Ninety-seven pieces of the man is all they found.

CHORUS

4. He gave it to a pirate who was sailin' east;
   The pirate stuffed him in a sack and added some yeast.
   He thought the extra weight would make him sink like a stone;
   But the yeast began to rise and it floated him home.

CHORUS

(Slower . . .)

5. They say that cats are clever;
   They say they have nine lives,
   They say that cats are bad luck,
   They scratch and claw and fight.
   We'd like to tell you more of this poor man and his sad plight;
   But if we tried to tell it all it just might take all night.

CHORUS

Illustrations by Sally Schaedler © Susan Striker

A(TIVITY #4

The Boy Who Drew Cats is based on the story of the artist Sesshu Toyo. He had no art supplies, so he drew with charcoal left over from the fire. Try a charcoal drawing of cats for yourself. Imagine they are alive. It can be fun to add green glitter to the eyes. Just put a dab of glue in the eyeball and sprinkle glitter over it. Allow to dry.

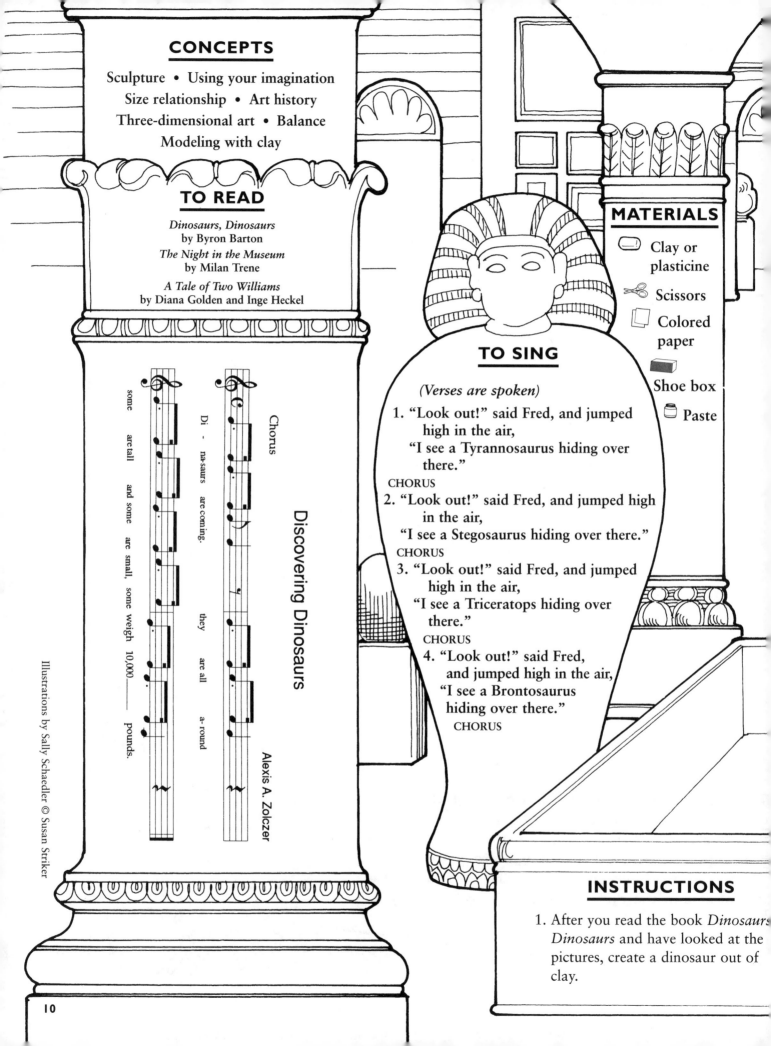

CONCEPTS

Sculpture • Using your imagination
Size relationship • Art history
Three-dimensional art • Balance
Modeling with clay

TO READ

Dinosaurs, Dinosaurs
by Byron Barton
The Night in the Museum
by Milan Trene

A Tale of Two Williams
by Diana Golden and Inge Heckel

Illustrations by Sally Schaedler © Susan Striker

Discovering Dinosaurs

Alexis A. Zolczer

Chorus

Di - na-saurs are coming.   they are all   a-round

some   are tall   and some   are small, some weigh 10,000 ——— pounds.

MATERIALS

Clay or plasticine

Scissors

Colored paper

Shoe box

Paste

TO SING

(Verses are spoken)

1. "Look out!" said Fred, and jumped high in the air,
   "I see a Tyrannosaurus hiding over there."
   CHORUS
2. "Look out!" said Fred, and jumped high in the air,
   "I see a Stegosaurus hiding over there."
   CHORUS
3. "Look out!" said Fred, and jumped high in the air,
   "I see a Triceratops hiding over there."
   CHORUS
4. "Look out!" said Fred, and jumped high in the air,
   "I see a Brontosaurus hiding over there."
   CHORUS

INSTRUCTIONS

1. After you read the book *Dinosaurs, Dinosaurs* and have looked at the pictures, create a dinosaur out of clay.

10

ACTIVITY #5

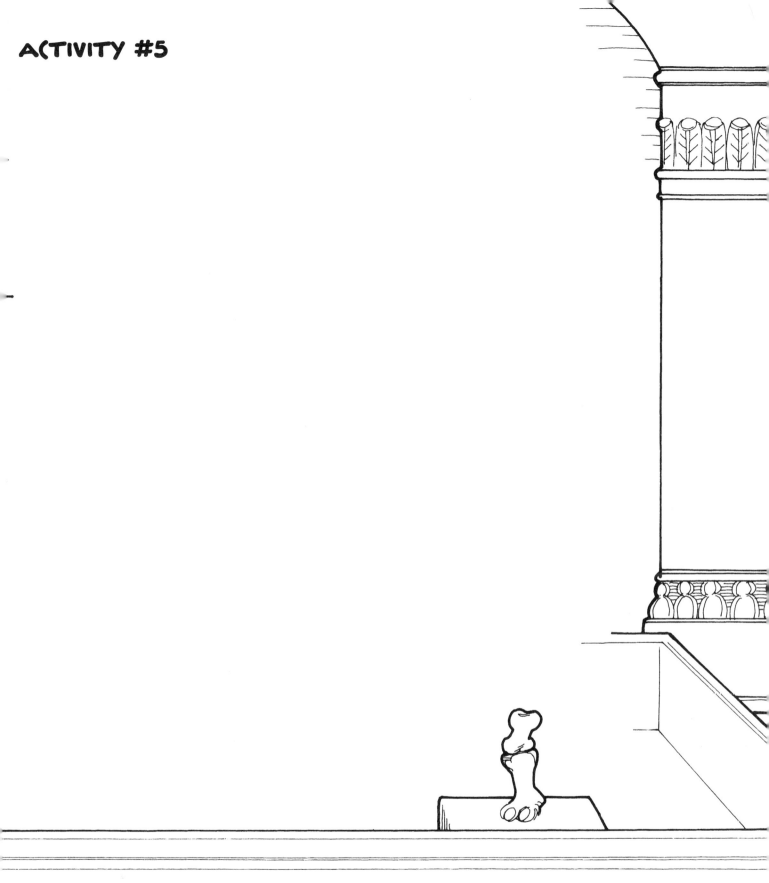

2. While waiting for clay to dry or be fired, create a diorama. Using an old shoe box and colored papers, create an appropriate environment for a dinosaur to live in. Consider scale—how big was a dinosaur compared to a tree?

You are the leader of a team of paleontologists who have brought back bones and are reconstructing a newly discovered dinosaur to put on display at the Museum of Natural History.

Illustrations by Sally Schaedler © Susan Striker

TO SING

Where Has My Little Dog Gone

German Folk Song

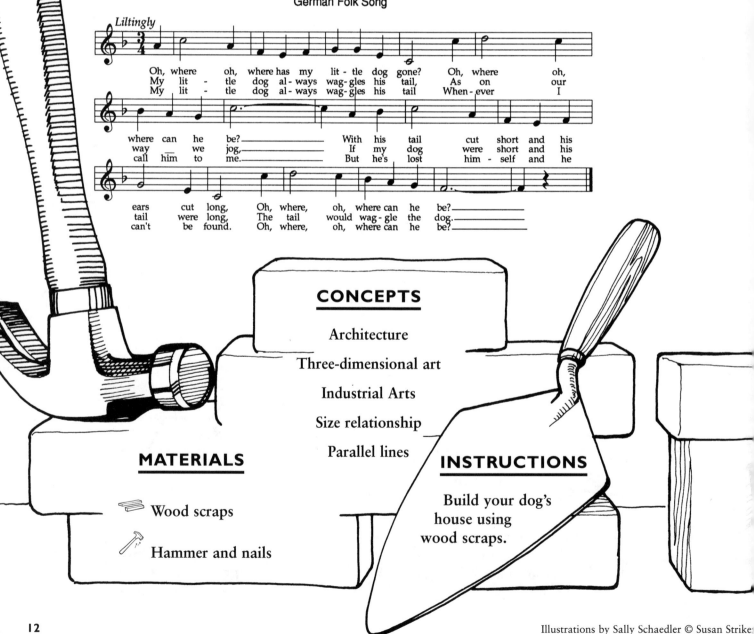

Liltingly

Oh, where oh, where has my lit - tle dog gone? Oh, where oh,
My lit - tle dog al - ways wag-gles his tail, As on our
My lit - tle dog al - ways wag-gles his tail When - ever I

where can he be?_____ With his tail cut short and his
way we jog,_____ If my dog were short and his
call him to me._____ But he's lost him - self and he

ears cut long, Oh, where, oh, where can he be?_____
tail were long, The tail would wag - gle the dog._____
can't be found. Oh, where, oh, where can he be?_____

CONCEPTS

Architecture

Three-dimensional art

Industrial Arts

Size relationship

Parallel lines

MATERIALS

Wood scraps

Hammer and nails

INSTRUCTIONS

Build your dog's house using wood scraps.

Illustrations by Sally Schaedler © Susan Strike

TO READ

Frankie's Bau-Wau Haus by Melanie Brown and Anthony Lawler

Spot a Dog, a Child's Book of Art by Lucy Micklethwait

A Home for Spooky
   by Gloria Rand and
   illustrated by Ted Rand

Lassie Come Home
   by Rosemary Wells and Susan Jeffers

The world's greatest architect has designed a doghouse for your favorite dog.

Illustrations by Sally Schaedler © Susan Striker

13

CONCEPTS

Using your imagination

Group work

TO READ

The Shelf Paper Jungle
by Diana Engel

The Peaceable Kingdom
by Ewa Zadrzynska

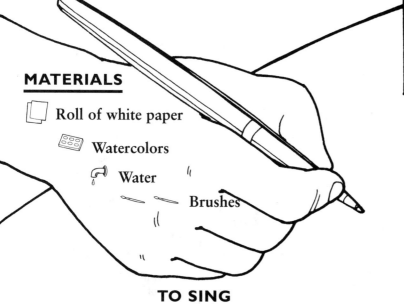

MATERIALS

☐ Roll of white paper

▦ Watercolors

⌔ Water

Brushes

TO SING

The Lion Sleeps Tonight

New Lyric and Revised Music by Hugo Peretti, Luigi Creatore, George Weiss, and Albert Stanton. Based on a Song by Solomon Linda and Paul Campbell

A(TIVITY #7A

Draw a shelf paper jungle with your friend.

A(TIVITY #7B

Create a paper animal.

CONCEPTS

Pasting

Cutting paper

Curling paper

INSTRUCTIONS

Read the book *The Shelf Paper Jungle* or *The Peaceable Kingdom*.

Work with one or more friends to paint an imaginary world of your own. Share all areas of the paper.

When completed, divide the mural and cut it up so that each friend takes a part home.

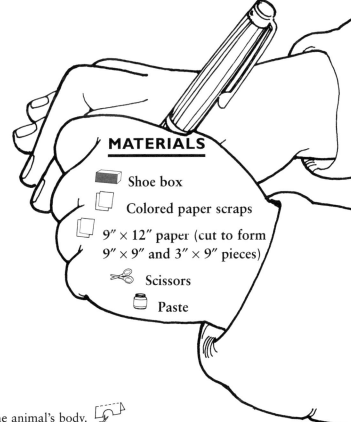

MATERIALS

▪ Shoe box

▢ Colored paper scraps

▢ 9″ × 12″ paper (cut to form 9″ × 9″ and 3″ × 9″ pieces)

✂ Scissors

▯ Paste

INSTRUCTIONS

1. Turn a shoe box on its side.

2. Cut and fold colored paper to create grass, trees, and jungle growth.

3. Fold 9″ × 9″ paper in half. Cut out half circle near center. This will be the animal's body.

4. Cut 3″ × 9″ strip into narrower strips. Curl by placing strip over sharp end of scissors, placing thumb over top of paper, and pulling. (Use for tail, whiskers, or other hair.) Paste on.

5. Decorate circle created in step 3 as an animal head.

6. Use a small scrap of paper folded like an accordion to attach head to body.

7. Decorate animal with distinctive details, such as spots, whiskers, claws, etc.

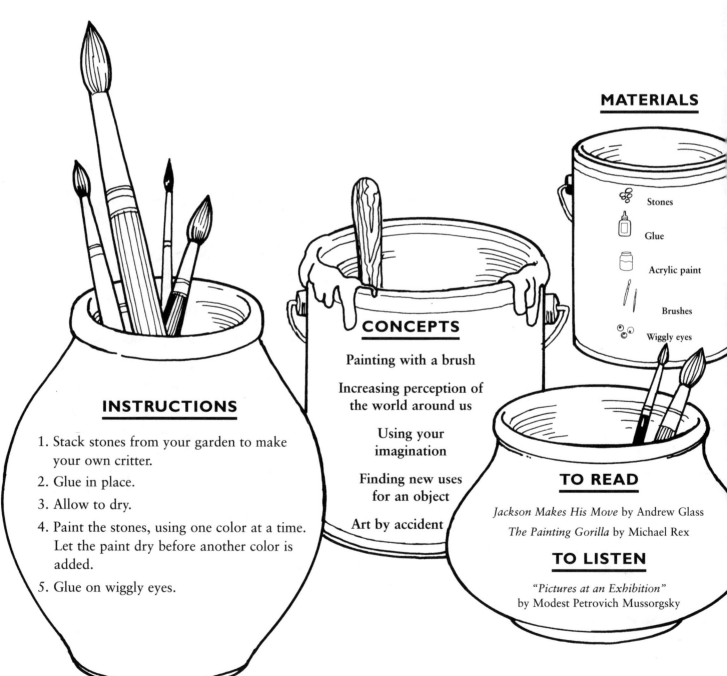

MATERIALS

Stones

Glue

Acrylic paint

Brushes

Wiggly eyes

CONCEPTS

Painting with a brush

Increasing perception of the world around us

Using your imagination

Finding new uses for an object

Art by accident

INSTRUCTIONS

1. Stack stones from your garden to make your own critter.
2. Glue in place.
3. Allow to dry.
4. Paint the stones, using one color at a time. Let the paint dry before another color is added.
5. Glue on wiggly eyes.

TO READ

Jackson Makes His Move by Andrew Glass

The Painting Gorilla by Michael Rex

TO LISTEN

"Pictures at an Exhibition" by Modest Petrovich Mussorgsky

Jackson Makes His Move tells the story of a raccoon who becomes a great abstract expressionist painter.

If a monkey could paint, what would the paintings look like?

A(TIVITY #9A

CONCEPTS

Using your imagination

Sewing

Pattern

Crafts

Write a list poem in the shape of a snake. In it, describe your snake and tell how you fe about it.

Use color words, texture words, and words with an *ssss* sound.

TO READ

Baby Rattlesnake
adapted by Lynn Moroney

The Snake Book
written and edited by Mary Ling and Mary Atkinson

INSTRUCTIONS

1. Read *Baby Rattlesnake* or *The Snake Book*.
2. Stuff pantyhose leg with fiberfill.
3. Secure open end with rubber band.
4. Fold over foot end of hose and make a few stitches at each corner to create snake's mouth.
5. Paint snake's skin.
6. If you wish, add wiggly eyes and decorate with "jewels."

(This project can be changed to create a great lizard, terrific octopus, etc. Use your imagination!)

MATERIALS

Leg cut from an old, clean pair of pantyhose

Fiberfill

Rubber band

Brushes

Needle and thread

Acrylic paint

Water

Optional:

"jewels"

wiggly eyes   glue

Illustrations by Sally Schaedler © Susan Striker

I'm Being Eaten by a Boa Constrictor

I'm be-ing eat-en by a bo-a con - strict - or!

TO SING

(Spoken)

Oh no, he's got my toe!
Oh gee, he's got my knee!
Oh my, he's got my thigh!
Oh yip, he's got my hip!
Make haste, he's got my waist!
Be calm, he's got my arm!
That's grand, he's got my hand!
That bum, he's got my thumb!
Oh yes, he's got my chest!
Oh heck, he's got my neck!
Hey, Ted, he's got my head!

(Strangling)

Hemahonahoomangragh . . .

ACTIVITY #9B

MATERIALS

- Self-hardening clay
- Acrylic paint
- Brushes
- Water

CONCEPTS

Clay coil
Modeling with clay
Painting with a brush

INSTRUCTIONS

1. Roll a coil of clay for snake.
2. Make mouth and eyes.
3. Allow to dry.
4. Paint.

Snakes are enchanted by the music and rhythmic movements of the snake charmer.

Illustrations by Sally Schaedler © Susan Striker

TO SING

Magic Feathers

Adapted Chippewa Song

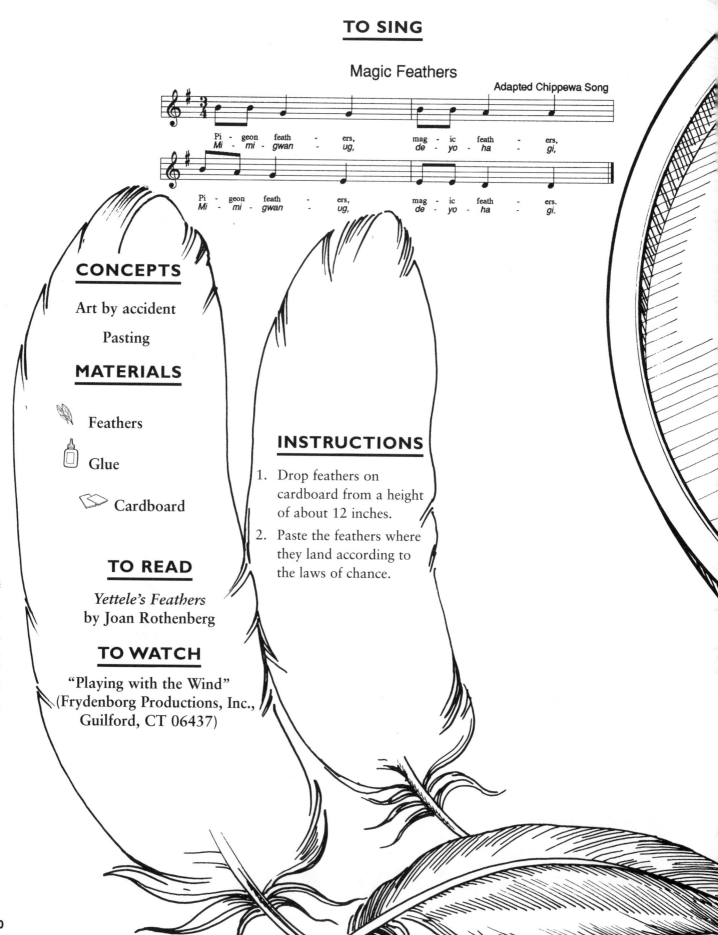

Pi - geon feath - ers, mag - ic feath - ers,
Mi - mi - gwan - ug, de - yo - ha - gi,

Pi - geon feath - ers, mag - ic feath - ers.
Mi - mi - gwan - ug, de - yo - ha - gi.

CONCEPTS

Art by accident

Pasting

MATERIALS

Feathers

Glue

Cardboard

TO READ

Yettele's Feathers
by Joan Rothenberg

TO WATCH

"Playing with the Wind"
(Frydenborg Productions, Inc.,
Guilford, CT 06437)

INSTRUCTIONS

1. Drop feathers on cardboard from a height of about 12 inches.

2. Paste the feathers where they land according to the laws of chance.

Hold a feather under a magnifying glass and draw what you see.

21

CONCEPTS

Cutting identical shapes

Increasing perception of the world around us

Paper-folding techniques

Cutting paper

Pasting

MATERIALS

Colored paper

Feathers

Scissors

Paste

Hole punch

Stapler

Thread or yarn

TO SING

Alouette

French Canadian Folk Song

Refrain   *Fine*

A - lou et - te,   gen - tille A-lou-et - te,   A - lou-et - te,   je te plu - me-rai.

Verse

Leader   *Group*

1. Je   te plu - me rai   la tête,   Je   te plu - me-rai   la tête,
2. Je   te plu - me rai   le bec,   Je   te plu - me-rai   le bec,

Leader   *Group*   *D. C. al Fine*

Et   la tête,   et   la tête,   A - lou-ette,   A - lou-ette.   Oh!
Et   le bec,   et   le bec,   A - lou-ette,   A - lou-ette.   Oh!
Et   la tête,   et   la tête.

TO READ

Paper Bird
by Arcadio Lobato

Our Yard Is Full of Birds
by Anne Rockwell

Feathers for Lunch
by Lois Ehlert

INSTRUCTIONS

1. Fold colored paper in half.

2. Draw a bird's body.

3. Cut out, making sure not to cut off the fold.

4. Holding both sides together, cut out eyes, markings, etc.

5. Paste one eye on each side of the bird's body.

6. Paste two beaks together.

7. Staple both sides of tail together.

8. Add feathers and markings.

9. Punch a hole in top of bird and string thread or yarn through it to hang it out of the way of the hungry cat!

TO LISTEN

"Peter and the Wolf"
by Sergei Prokofiev

22

Illustrations by Sally Schaedler

© Susan Striker

Make sure your bird can fly up high so the cat can't catch it.

Illustrations by Sally Schaedler © Susan Striker

23

CONCEPTS

Sculpture: Removing

Increasing perception of the world around us

MATERIALS

Soft wood

Whittling knife

Paint

Brushes

TO READ

Tales of Tutu, Nene and Nele by Gales Bates

TO SING

Go Tell Aunt Rhody

American Folk Song

1.Go tell Aunt Rhody - y, Go tell Aunt Rhod - y,
2.The one she's been sav - ing.The one she's been sav - ing.The
3.She died in a mill pond.She died in a mill pond.She
4.The gos - lings are cry - ing.The gos - lings are cry - ing.The

Go tell Aunt Rhod - y Her old grey goose is dead.
one she's been sav - ing To make a feath - er bed.
died in a mill pond Stand - ing on her head.
gos - lings are cry - ing The old gray goose is dead.

INSTRUCTIONS

1. Read the book *Tales of Tutu, Nene and Nele* or look at other pictures of geese.

2. Look at wood carved decoys and discuss their function. Think about how we can fool a hunter or predator by showing the decoy instead of the real bird.

3. Carve a bird's body.

4. Paint features, eyes, other details.

Everyone enjoys looking at the geese as they swim in the canal.

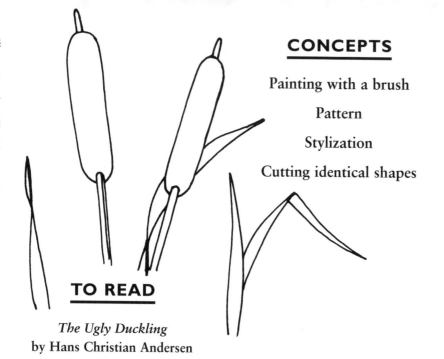

CONCEPTS

Painting with a brush

Pattern

Stylization

Cutting identical shapes

TO READ

The Ugly Duckling
by Hans Christian Andersen

Why Ducks Sleep on One Leg
by Sherry Garland

MATERIALS

15″ × 18″ white paper

Tempera or watercolor paint

Scissors   Brushes

Stapler   Newspaper

String

INSTRUCTIONS

1. Look at pictures of birds.

2. Hold two sheets of paper together as if they were one sheet, and cut out a bird shape.

3. Place two birds, facing each other, on the table.

4. Paint eyes, feathers, claws, etc., on the first bird and repeat on the second.

5. Hold birds together, decorated sides out, and staple around the edges, leaving a small area open to allow room to stuff.

6. Stuff evenly with crumpled newspaper.

7. Staple open edges together.

8. Attach string so that bird can be hung from the ceiling.

TO SING

Six Little Ducks

Six lit-tle ducks that I once knew;
Fat ones, skin-ny ones, they were too,
But the one lit-tle duck with the fea-ther on his back,
He ruled the o-thers with his "Quack quack quack!
Quack quack quack!" He ruled the o-thers with his "Quack quack quack!"

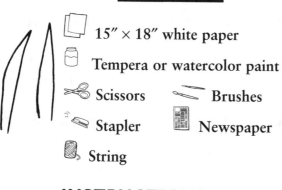

**The ducks are all laughing
at the ugly duckling.**

Illustrations by Sally Schaedler © Susan Striker

CONCEPTS

Crafts

Texture

Using your imagination

MATERIALS

Cardboard for background

White glue

Black yarn

Colored yarn scraps

TO READ

Tanglebird
by Bernard Lodge

The Art of the Birdhouse
Flights of Fancy
by Mike Dillon
and Jim Linna

INSTRUCTIONS

1. Draw a picture of a bird on cardboard.
2. Outline the bird with white glue.
3. Press black yarn over the glue.
4. Spread glue in open spaces and fill with colored yarn, spiraling yarn from center until it completely fills space.

ACTIVITY #14B

CONCEPTS

Weaving

Concentric shapes

Increase perception of the world around us

MATERIALS

Cardboard

Grasses, twigs, leaves

Scissors

Pencils

INSTRUCTIONS

1. Draw two circles, one inside the other, on cardboard.
2. Cut out inverted V shapes from the outer edge to the inner circle.
3. Fold the remaining cardboard up from the center.
4. Use the cardboard to weave your own bird's nest, using as many natural materials as possible.

TO SING

Bird Nest

by Barbara J. Hawkins

A bird can build a nest from things we hard-ly see, He finds them on the ground and puts them in his tree, He then be-gins to weave as qui-et as a mouse And be-fore you know what's hap-pened, he has a lit-tle house.

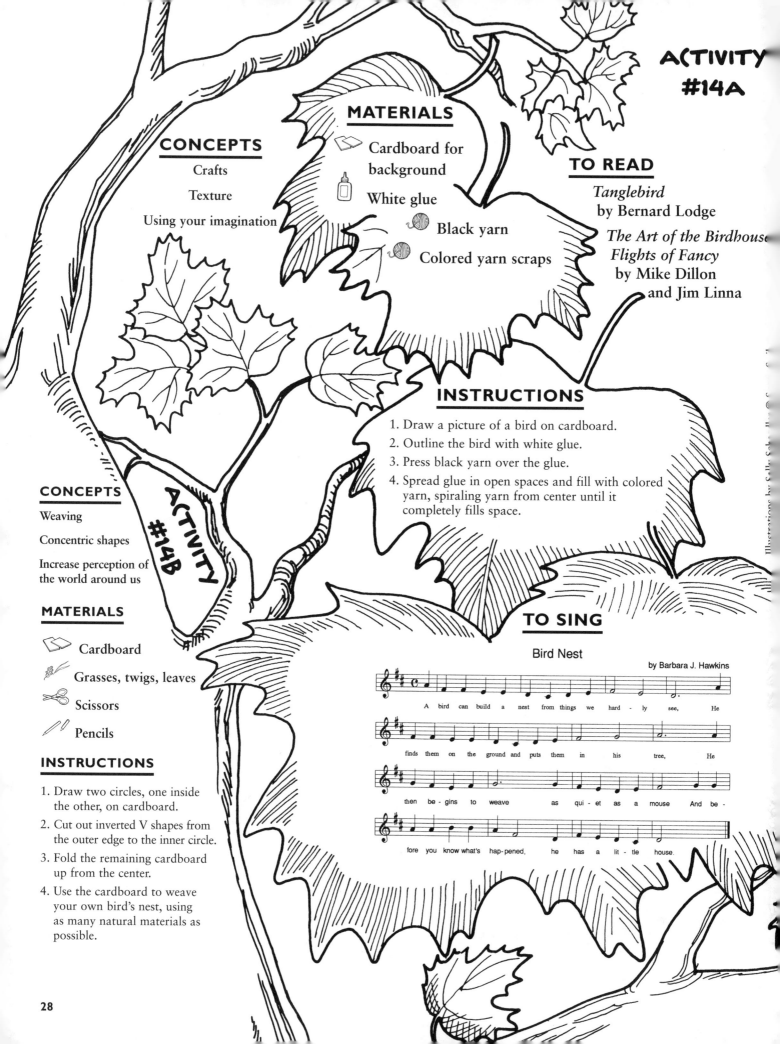

A new baby bird just hatched and surprised everyone!

Illustrations by Sally Schaedler © Susan Striker

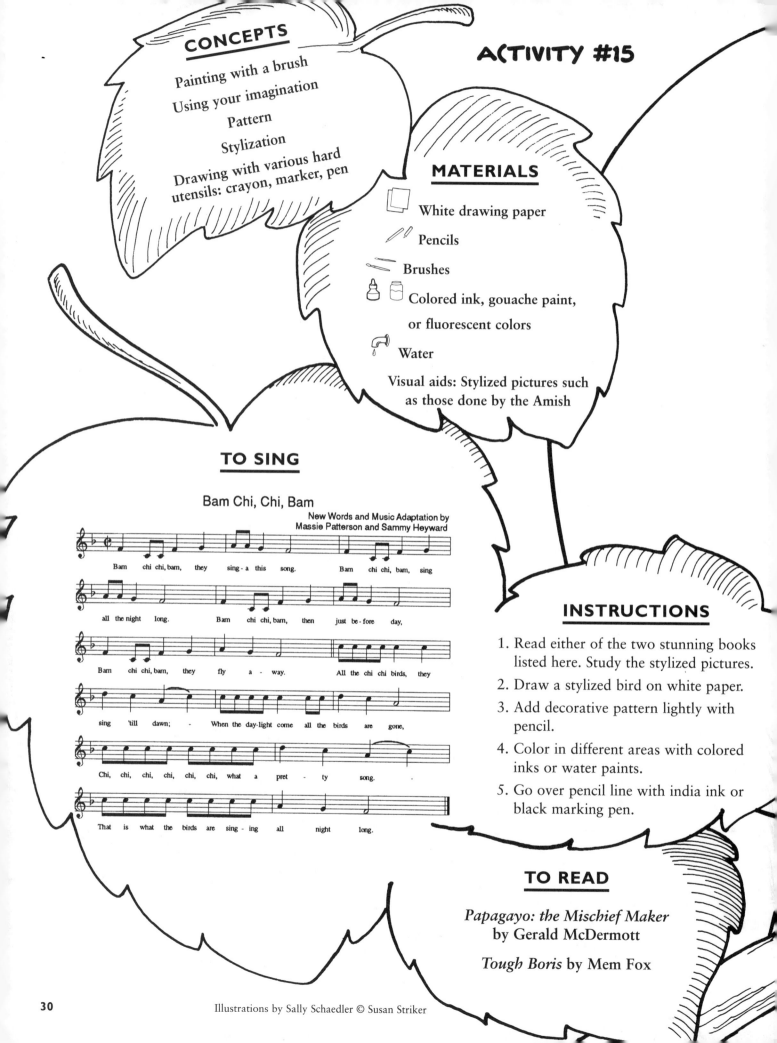

CONCEPTS

Painting with a brush

Using your imagination

Pattern

Stylization

Drawing with various hard utensils: crayon, marker, pen

ACTIVITY #15

MATERIALS

White drawing paper

Pencils

Brushes

Colored ink, gouache paint, or fluorescent colors

Water

Visual aids: Stylized pictures such as those done by the Amish

TO SING

Bam Chi, Chi, Bam

New Words and Music Adaptation by
Massie Patterson and Sammy Heyward

Bam chi chi, bam, they sing-a this song. Bam chi chi, bam, sing all the night long. Bam chi chi, bam, then just be-fore day, Bam chi chi, bam, they fly a-way. All the chi chi birds, they sing 'till dawn; — When the day-light come all the birds are gone, Chi, chi, chi, chi, chi, chi, what a pret-ty song. That is what the birds are sing-ing all night long.

INSTRUCTIONS

1. Read either of the two stunning books listed here. Study the stylized pictures.
2. Draw a stylized bird on white paper.
3. Add decorative pattern lightly with pencil.
4. Color in different areas with colored inks or water paints.
5. Go over pencil line with india ink or black marking pen.

TO READ

Papagayo: the Mischief Maker by Gerald McDermott

Tough Boris by Mem Fox

Illustrations by Sally Schaedler © Susan Striker

This talkative parrot has a tall tale to tell.

Illustrations by Sally Schaedler © Susan Striker

You are the first person to see this rare and wonderful bird who lives deep in the rain forest.

Illustrations by Sally Schaedler © Susan Striker

TO SING

The Mocking Bird

Freely with expression

1.Hush, lit-tle ba - by, don't say a word, Pa-pa's gon-na buy you a mock-ing bird.

INSTRUCTIONS

1. Draw shape of a bird on paper, eliminating all details.
2. Cut out shape.
3. Pin pattern through two thicknesses of felt or fabric.
4. Sew two sheets of fabric together, using a backstitch. Leave a small opening.
6. Turn bird inside out and stuff with the fiberfill.
7. Tuck in edges of opening; sew closed.
8. Sew or glue on details such as feathers, claws, or eyes.

TO READ

Little Birds, Big Birds
by Henry Mangione

King of the Birds
by Helen Ward

CONCEPTS

Cutting

Pasting

Sewing

Silhouette

Making and using
patterns

MATERIALS

Glue

Two 9″ × 12″ pieces of felt

9″ × 12″ paper

Pencils

Scissors

Needle and thread

Polyester fiberfill or fabric
scraps

Optional: feathers

ACTIVITY #17A

CONCEPTS

Optical illusions

Using soft drawing utensils:
charcoal, chalk, oil pastels

MATERIALS

Newsprint or other lightweight paper

Small oaktag

Scissors   Oil pastels

Illustrations by Sally Schaedler © Susan Striker

INSTRUCTIONS

1. Cut a bird out of oaktag.
2. Place the bird on the table.
3. Place newsprint over the bird, keeping bird near the edge of the paper.
4. Rub over figure with crayon.
5. Move oaktag bird slightly.
6. Rub again.
7. Repeat across entire page.

TO READ

Catskill Eagle by Herman Melville

Capturing Nature, the Writing and Art of John James Audubon
edited by Peter and Connie Roop

CONCEPTS

Increasing perception
of the world around us

Wax resist

ACTIVITY #17B

MATERIALS

Wax crayons

Light blue wash (one
cup water mixed with
one drop blue paint)

Brush

White paper

INSTRUCTIONS

1. Read the book *Catskill Eagle* and study examples of birds in flight.
2. Draw a bird with crayon, pressing hard so that the wax in the crayon adheres to the paper.
3. Cover entire paper with light blue wash.

Birds in flight are a delightful sight.

35

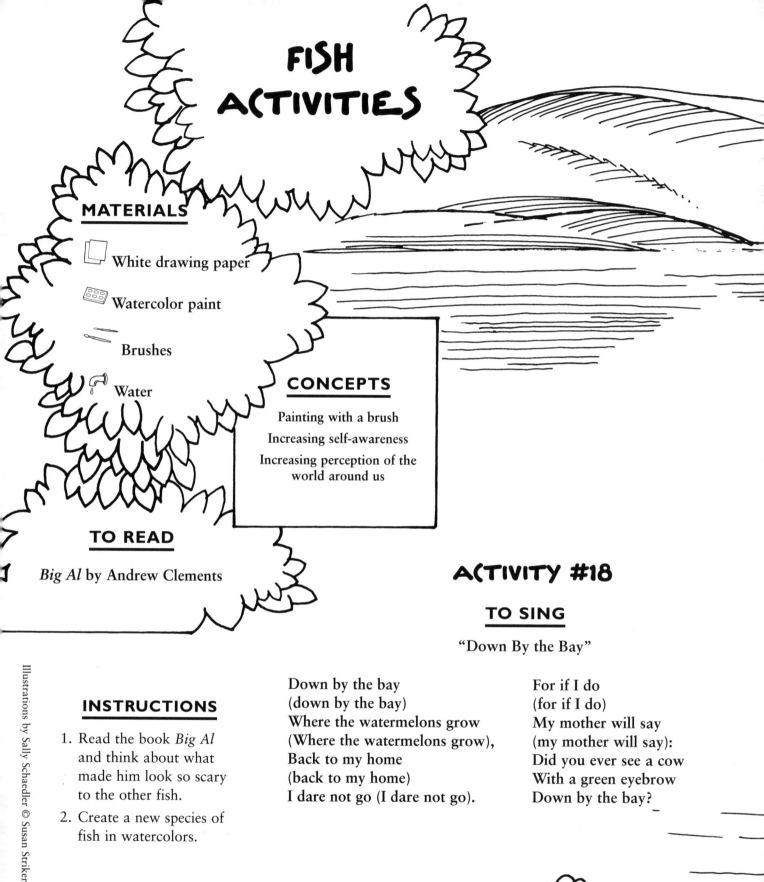

FISH ACTIVITIES

MATERIALS

White drawing paper

Watercolor paint

Brushes

Water

CONCEPTS

Painting with a brush

Increasing self-awareness

Increasing perception of the world around us

TO READ

Big Al by Andrew Clements

ACTIVITY #18

TO SING

"Down By the Bay"

INSTRUCTIONS

1. Read the book *Big Al* and think about what made him look so scary to the other fish.

2. Create a new species of fish in watercolors.

Down by the bay
(down by the bay)
Where the watermelons grow
(Where the watermelons grow),
Back to my home
(back to my home)
I dare not go (I dare not go).

For if I do
(for if I do)
My mother will say
(my mother will say):
Did you ever see a cow
With a green eyebrow
Down by the bay?

An ugly monster fish has been sighted at your favorite swimming hole!

37

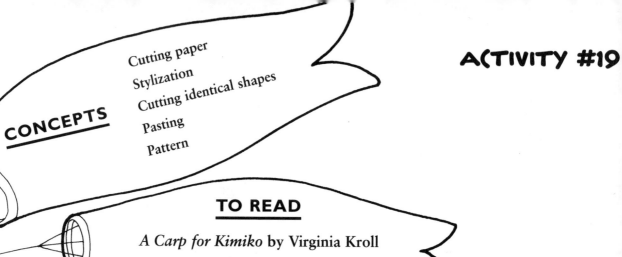

CONCEPTS

Cutting paper
Stylization
Cutting identical shapes
Pasting
Pattern

TO READ

A Carp for Kimiko by Virginia Kroll

MATERIALS

 Four sheets of
12″ × 18″ tissue paper

 Scissors

 Paste

 Reed or wire,
approximately 10″ long

 Masking tape

String

INSTRUCTIONS

1. Read the book *A Carp for Kimiko*.

2. To create a Japanese-style fish kite, hold all four sheets of tissue together and cut out the shape of a fish.

3. Paste edges of all four sheets together at top, bottom, and tail. Do not paste mouth.

4. Decorate front and back of fish with tissue paper scraps.

5. Tape reed or wire into a circle.

6. Insert reed or wire into fish mouth.

7. Attach kite string to reed or wire.

Illustrations by Sally Schaedler © Susan Striker

**Fly a fish kite in Japan
on Children's Day.**

39

ACTIVITY #20

TO READ

In the Swim: Poems and Paintings
by Douglas Florian

Blue Sea by Robert Kalan

TO SING

There's a Hole in the Middle of the Sea

Anonymous

1. There's a hole in the mid-dle of the sea,

There's a hole in the mid-dle of the sea,

There's a hole,——————— There's a hole,

There's a hole in the mid-dle of the sea.

2. There's a log in the hole in the middle of the sea.
3. There's a bump on the log in the hole in the middle of the sea.
4. There's a frog on the bump on the log in the hole in the middle of the sea.
5. There's a fly on the frog on the bump on the log in the hole in the middle of the sea.
6. There's a wing on the fly on the frog on the bump on the log in the hole in the middle of the sea.
7. There's a flea on the wing on the fly on the frog on the bump on the log in the hole in the middle of the sea.

MATERIALS

- Styrofoam meat tray
- Colored tissue paper
- Double-sided, self-adhesive foam circles
- Oaktag
- Markers
- Diluted white glue

INSTRUCTIONS

1. Cut or tear tissue in shapes of seaweed, coral, etc.
2. Paste tissue onto Styrofoam tray, over-lapping to create new colors.
3. Draw a fish on oak-tag. Cut it out and decorate it.
4. Use foam circles to paste fish in tray for 3-D effect.

CONCEPTS

Color mixing
Pasting

40 Illustrations by Sally Schaedler © Susan Striker

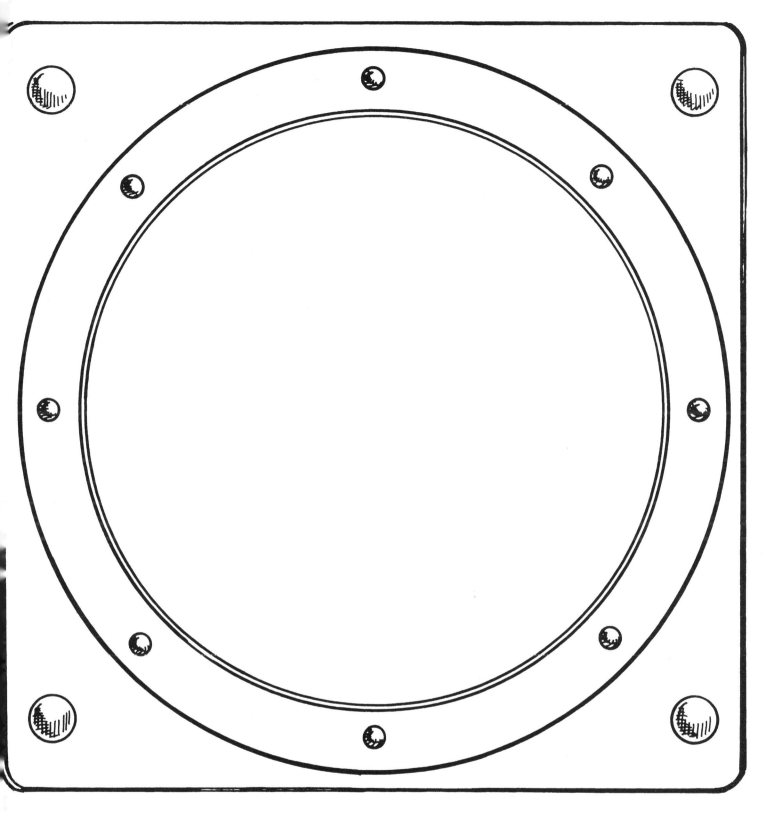

On your very own boat, you have a private porthole for viewing a very special world.

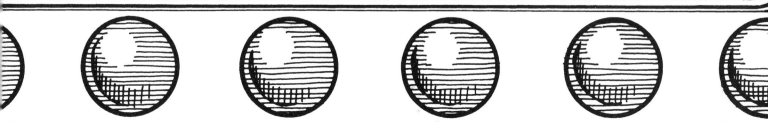

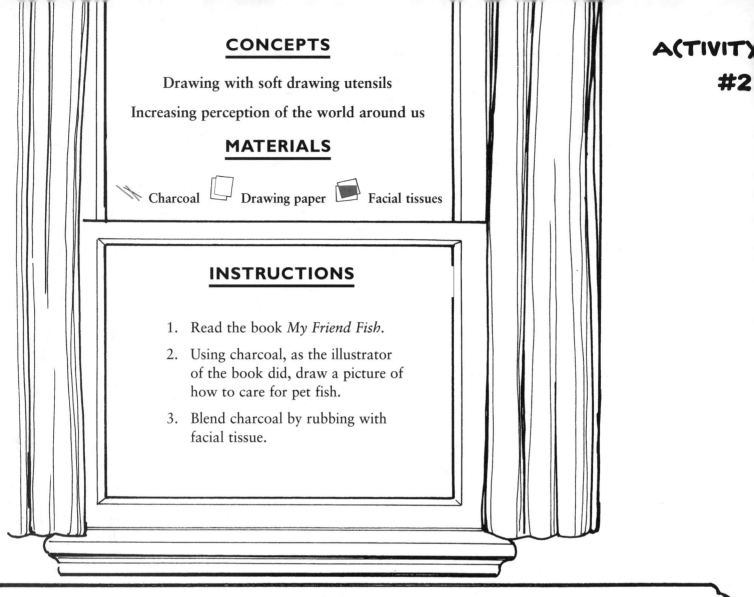

CONCEPTS

Drawing with soft drawing utensils

Increasing perception of the world around us

MATERIALS

Charcoal   Drawing paper   Facial tissues

INSTRUCTIONS

1. Read the book *My Friend Fish*.

2. Using charcoal, as the illustrator of the book did, draw a picture of how to care for pet fish.

3. Blend charcoal by rubbing with facial tissue.

TO SING

I've a Pair of Fishes

Jewish Folk Tune
Words by J. Lilian Vandevere

1. I've a pair of fish - es, fish - es. They are wash-ing dish - es, dish - es. This is in-
2. I've a pair of fox - es, fox - es. They are build-ing box - es, box - es. This is in-

deed a won-der. See the fish-es washing dish-es. This is quite a won - der, This is quite a won - der.
deed a won-der. See the fox-es building box-es. This is quite a won - der, This is quite a won - der.

TO READ

My Friend Fish
by Mamie Hagwood

If you had your own fish, how would you take care of it?

Illustrations by Sally Schaedler © Susan Striker

43

ACTIVITY #22

MATERIALS

- Fresh, whole fish with skin on
  OR
- Life/Form Replicas of Fish (NASCO, P.O. Box 901, Fort Atkinson, WI 53538-0901)

- Nontoxic water-soluble ink or tempera paint
- Drawing paper
- Brushes
- Water

TO READ

A River Dream
by Allen Say

TO SING

Song of the Fishes

Sea Chantey

1. Come, all ye young sail-or-men, lis-ten to me,— I'll sing you a song of the fish of the sea.
2. Oh, first came the whale— the big gest of all,— He climbed up a-loft and let ev-ery sail fall.

Refrain

Then blow, ye winds west-er-ly, west-er-ly, blow,—We're bound to the south-'ard, so stead-y she goes!

INSTRUCTIONS

1. A Japanese folk tale says that the art of Gyotaku (fish printing) began so that a fisher-man could compete for the honor of proving that the fish he caught, and subsequently cut and cleaned, was the biggest catch of the day.

2. Apply ink to fish.

3. Place the fish on paper and gently rock it from side to side, spreading out the tail and fins.

4. If you thoroughly wash and cook the fish, it may be safely eaten.

CONCEPTS

Increasing perception of the world around us

Cultural diversity

Printing

Art history

Texture

Pattern

Illustrations by Sally Schaedler © Susan Striker

This time you caught a fantastic and wonderful surprise!

ACTIVITY #23

Illustrations by Sally Schaedler © Susan Striker

CONCEPTS

Increasing perception of
the world around us

Balance

Modeling with clay

MATERIALS

Water

Air-drying clay

Clay tool

Acrylic paint

INSTRUCTIONS

1. Read the book *Fish Faces* and observe the fish and plant life.
2. Model a fish from clay.
3. Create an ocean floor and plant life that can be joined to the fish to support it.
4. Connect fish to ocean floor and plant life by scoring both, applying slip, and melding to secure a bond.
5. Allow to dry.
6. Paint.

TO LISTEN

"Carnival of Animals"
by Camille Saint-Saëns

TO SING

"There Was an Old Fish"

I'm going home. I've got a home up
  yonder.
A few days and a few days,
I've got a home up yonder and I'm
  going home.
Swam the ocean 'round and 'round,
A few days and a few days,
Spewed out Jonah on dry ground,
  And I'm going home.

Illustrations by Sally Schaedler © Susan Striker

TO READ

Fish Faces by Norbert Wu

The Sweet and Sour Animal Book by Langston Hughes

Out of the Ocean by Debra Frasier

For a scuba diver, every dive provides thrilling and exciting discoveries.

ACTIVITY #24

CONCEPTS

Increasing self-awareness
Increasing perception of the
world around us
Analogous colors

MATERIALS

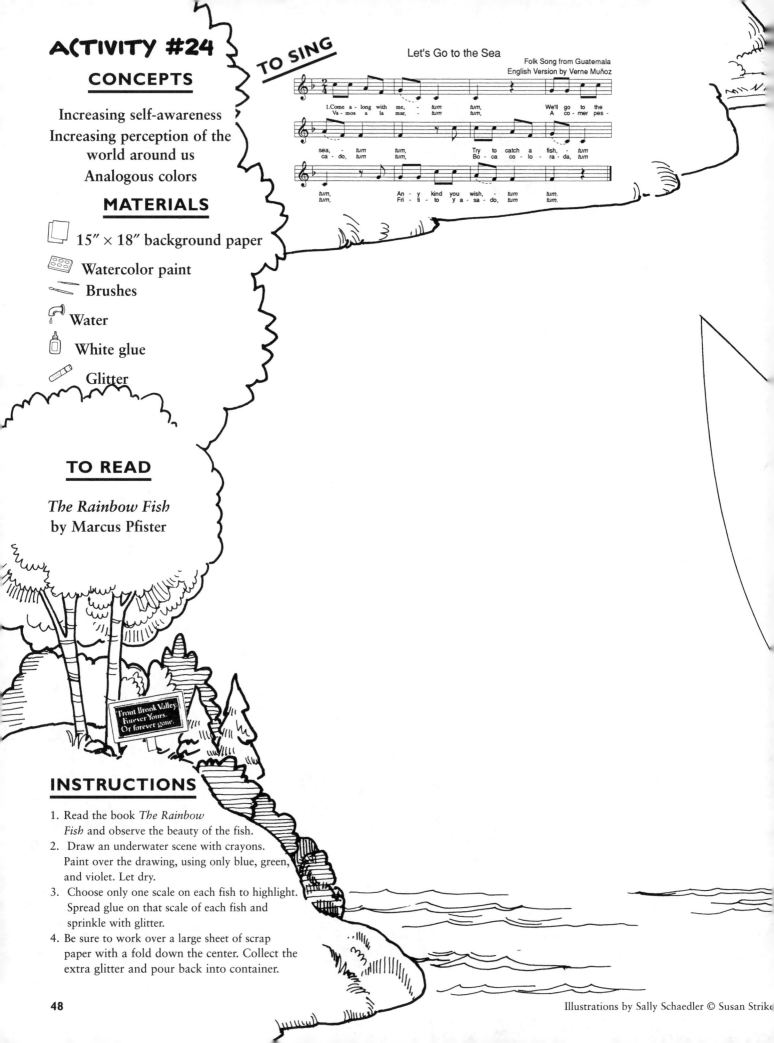

15″ × 18″ background paper

Watercolor paint

Brushes

Water

White glue

Glitter

TO SING

Let's Go to the Sea

Folk Song from Guatemala
English Version by Verne Muñoz

1.Come a - long with me, - tum tum, We'll go to the
Va - mos a la mar, - tum tum, A co - mer pes -

sea, - tum tum, Try to catch a fish, - tum
ca - do, tum tum, Bo - ca co - lo - ra - da, tum

tum, An - y kind you wish, - tum tum.
tum, Fri - ti - to y a - sa - do, tum tum.

TO READ

The Rainbow Fish
by Marcus Pfister

Trout Brook Valley.
Forever Yours.
Or forever gone.

INSTRUCTIONS

1. Read the book *The Rainbow
   Fish* and observe the beauty of the fish.
2. Draw an underwater scene with crayons.
   Paint over the drawing, using only blue, green,
   and violet. Let dry.
3. Choose only one scale on each fish to highlight.
   Spread glue on that scale of each fish and
   sprinkle with glitter.
4. Be sure to work over a large sheet of scrap
   paper with a fold down the center. Collect the
   extra glitter and pour back into container.

48

Illustrations by Sally Schaedler © Susan Strike

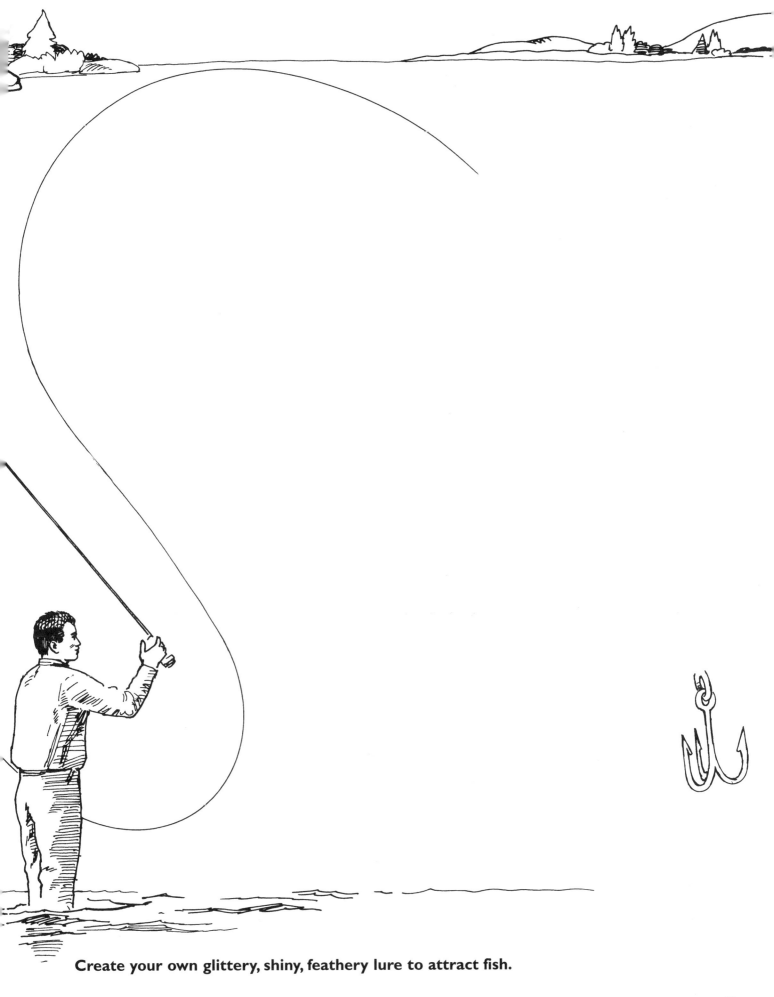

Create your own glittery, shiny, feathery lure to attract fish.

Illustrations by Sally Schaedler © Susan Striker

CONCEPTS

Distortion

Color mixing

Close up views

Increasing perception
of the world around us

MATERIALS

Watercolor paint

Brushes

15″ × 18″ paper

Crayons

Scissors

Visual Aids: Pictures of tropical fish

INSTRUCTIONS

1. Read the book *Into the Sea or My Camera at the Aquarium*.

2. If possible, visit an aquarium to see tropical fish.

3. Consider being the proprietor of an aquarium that you have designed.

4. Cut paper into the shape of a fishbowl or tank.

5. Draw fish and other details with crayons.

6. Paint with colors that are reminiscent of water (such as blue, green, turquoise) in wide bands across the paper. Apply paint quickly so that the colors run together. Observe how the watercolors resist the wax in the crayons.

Can you imagine that while you are looking and talking about the fish at the aquarium, they are looking at and talking about you?

Illustrations by Sally Schaedler © Susan Striker

TO READ

Into the Sea
by Brenda Z. Guiberson

*My Camera at
the Aquarium*
by Janet Perry Marshall

Draw two fish in your aquarium. Write a conversation between them—observations about the humans on the other side of the glass. Use the cartoon-style speech bubbles above. **51**

ACTIVITY #26

INSTRUCTIONS

1. Think about the functions of tails, gills, and fins.
2. Observe decorative aspects of many different fish.
3. Hold two pieces of paper together. On top sheet, draw a fish. Cut fish out of both pieces of paper.
4. Draw four sets of parallel lines that can be curved, zigzagged, or vertical, or divide into geometric shapes that divide the fish into four equal parts.
5. Cut along lines through both sheets of paper to create four to six shapes that represent sections of a fish, such as the head, body sections, and tail.
6. Place shapes about one-half-inch apart in the order you want them to be placed.
7. Place a piece of string across all the sections.
8. With small pieces of tape, attach the string to each section of the fish.
9. Decorate both sides of the fish with cut paper scraps.
10. Tie one end of the string to a stick or pencil and the fish will look like it's swimming when you move it.

TO READ

Fish Is Fish by Leo Lionni

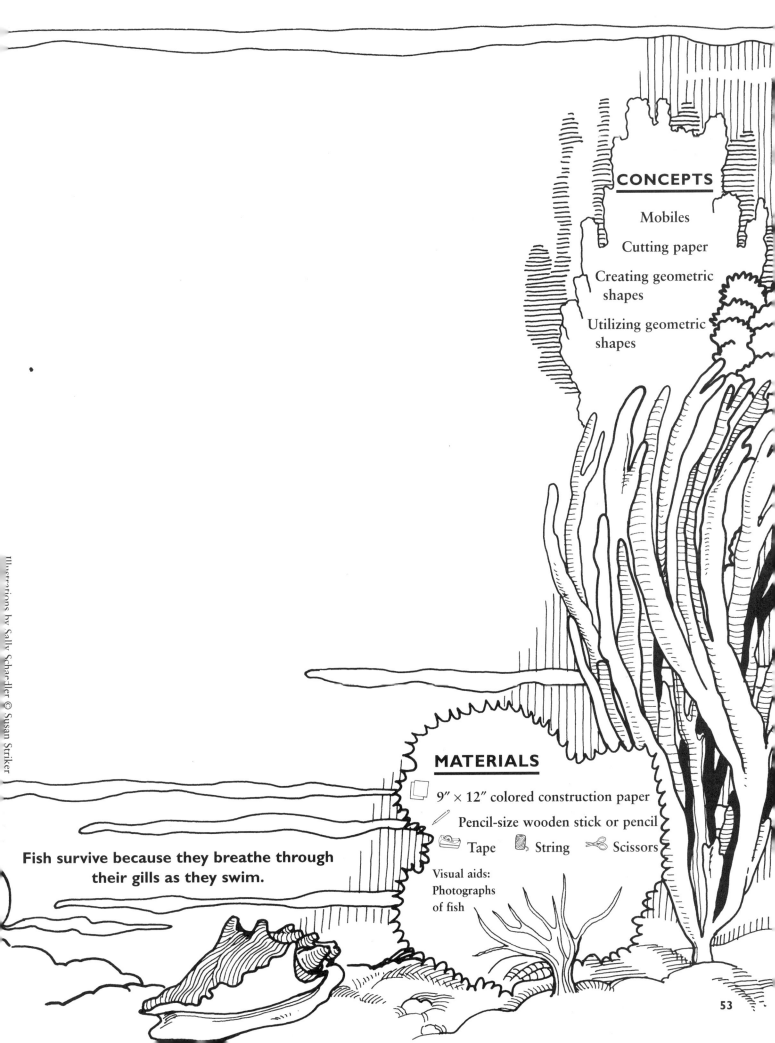

CONCEPTS

Mobiles

Cutting paper

Creating geometric shapes

Utilizing geometric shapes

MATERIALS

9" × 12" colored construction paper

Pencil-size wooden stick or pencil

Tape   String   Scissors

Visual aids:
Photographs
of fish

Fish survive because they breathe through their gills as they swim.

FLOWER ACTIVITIES

Illustrations by Sally Schaedler © Susan Strik

Create your own magic vase.

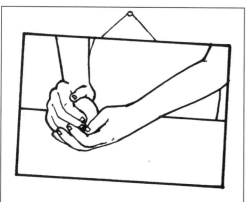

1. Make a ball of clay.

2. Flatten clay by pounding on it.

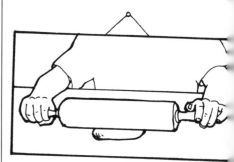

3. Using a rolling pin, roll it into a sla
   of even thickness.

4. Trace around a can and cut out to create a round bottom.

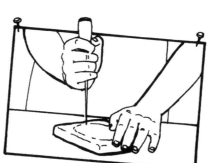

5. Roll out long, thin strips of clay,
   keeping your fingers spread apart.

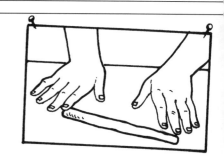

6. "Scratch and attach." Scratch both
   pot and coil where they will meet.
   Moisten with water, and with pres-
   sure attach coil to bottom of pot.

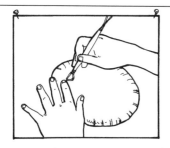

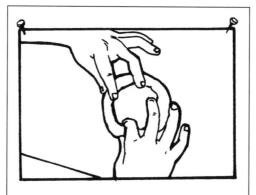

7. Continue attaching coils to each other.

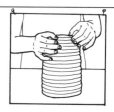

8. Smooth coils together on the inside a
   pot builds up in height. Allow to dry
9. Glaze and fire.
10. Create special flowers to put in you
    magic vase using paper, feathers, pipe
    cleaners, or other materials.

MATERIALS
Clay   Water
Ceramic glaze   White glue
Tempera paint

CONCEPTS
Clay coil

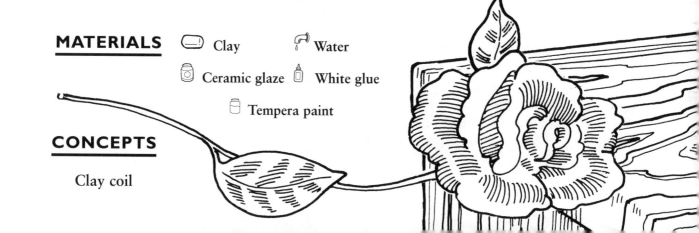

54

ACTIVITY #27

TO LISTEN

"Waltz of the Flowers" from *The Nutcracker Suite* by Tchaikovsky

Draw a bouquet of flowers for this magic vase.

TO READ

The Magic Vase by Fiona French

Illustrations by Sally Schaedler © Susan Striker   **55**

INSTRUCTIONS

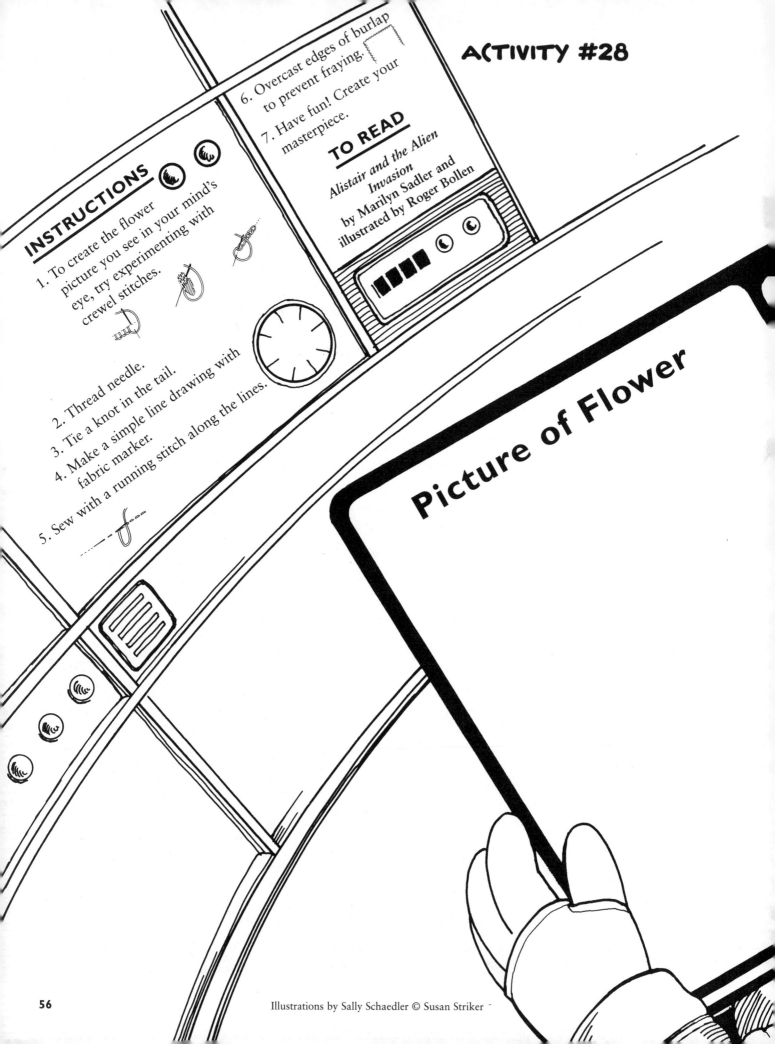

1. To create the flower picture you see in your mind's eye, try experimenting with crewel stitches.

2. Thread needle.

3. Tie a knot in the tail.

4. Make a simple line drawing with fabric marker.

5. Sew with a running stitch along the lines.

6. Overcast edges of burlap to prevent fraying.

7. Have fun! Create your masterpiece.

TO READ

Alistair and the Alien Invasion
by Marilyn Sadler and illustrated by Roger Bollen

Picture of Flower

Illustrations by Sally Schaedler © Susan Striker

roposed name of discovery:

Place discovered:

Unique characteristics:

Discovered by:

CONCEPTS
Sewing
Crafts

MATERIALS

Burlap

Crewel needles

Yarn

Fabric marker

You have been sent on a scientific expedition to bring back information about a newly discovered flower on another planet.

A(TIVITY #29A

TISSUE PAPER CARNATION

CONCEPTS

Paper-folding techniques

Three-dimensional art

MATERIALS

Pipe cleaner

One sheet green or brown paper

Five or six rectangular sheets of colored tissue paper

INSTRUCTIONS

1. Align all paper keeping green or brown paper on the bottom.

2. Fold like an accordion.

3. Secure in center with pipe cleaner.

4. Keeping green or brown on the bottom, begin to separate layers of tissue from the top to the bottom. Continue until every layer is separated.

5. Cut bottom green or brown layer to look like leaf petals.

A(TIVITY #29B

TISSUE PAPER ROSE

CONCEPTS

Paper-folding techniques

Three-dimensional art

MATERIALS

Four 5" tissue circles

Pipe cleaner

INSTRUCTIONS

1. Stack tissue circles.

2. Pinch in the center.

3. Separate tissue layers.

4. Twist pipe cleaner around base of flower.

TO SING

2. The prettiest limb you ever did see,
The limb was on the tree,
The tree was in the ground.
And the green grass grew all around,
all around
The green grass grew all around.

(continue similarly)

3. Now on this limb there grew a branch . .

4. Now on this branch there was a bough . .

5. Now on this bough there was a twig . . .

6. And on this twig there was a leaf . . .

7. And on this leaf there was a nest . . .

8. And in this nest there was an egg . . .

9. And in this egg there was a bird . . .

10. And on this bird there was a wing . . .

11. And on this wing there was a feather . . .

12. And on this feather there was a flea . . .

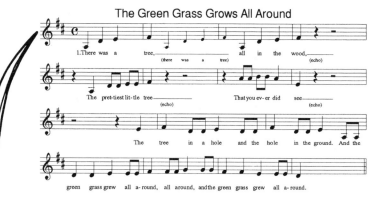

The Green Grass Grows All Around

1.There was a tree, (there was a tree) all in the wood, (echo)
The pret-tiest lit-tle tree (echo) That you ev- er did see, (echo)
The tree in a hole and the hole in the ground. And the
green grass grew all a-round, all around, and the green grass grew all a-round.

TO READ

In the Tall, Tall Grass
by Denise Fleming
"The Teeny-Tiny Woman" from
Fairy Tales and Fables, illustrated
by Gyo Fujikawa

58

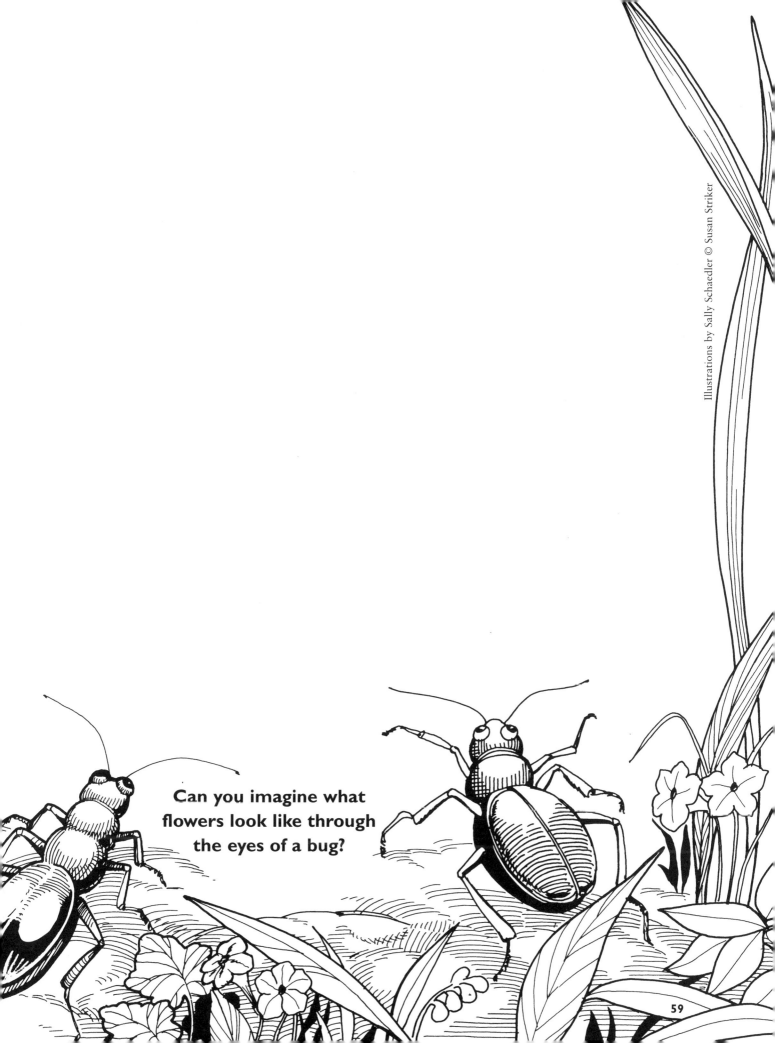

Can you imagine what flowers look like through the eyes of a bug?

CHALK FLOWER

CONCEPTS

Stylization

Using soft drawing utensils

Increasing perception of the world around us

INSTRUCTIONS

1. Read the book *The Gardener*.
2. Begin by drawing the center of a flower.
3. Use the side of the chalk in long, sweeping strokes to draw the petals radiating out from the center.
4. If desired, spray your drawing with fixative to preserve it.

MATERIALS

 Drawing paper   Chalk

TO READ

The Gardener
by Sarah Stewart,
illustrated by David Small

TO SING

Can You Plant the Seeds?
(Savez-vous planter les choux?)
Adapted Folk Song from France

1. Can you plant the gar - den seeds
French: Sa - vez - vous plant - er les choux,

Just as we do, just as we do?
A la mo - de, á la mo - de?

Can you plant the gar - den seeds
Sa - vez - vous plant - er les choux,

Just the same as we can do?
A la mo - de de chez nous?

POP-UP FLOWER GREETING CARD
INSTRUCTIONS

1. Read *The Poetry of Flowers*.
2. Fold square paper in half diagonally.
3. Cut off bottom corner.
4. Fold in two sides of the triangle to the back to make "wings."
5. Cut out shapes in body of triangle—similar to a snowflake.
6. Fold rectangular paper in half to create a card.
7. Tape wings of flower to card.

CONCEPTS

Cutting paper

Recognizing and naming geometric shapes

Creating geometric shapes

Paper-folding techniques

Three-dimensional art

MATERIALS

One square sheet of colored paper

One rectangular sheet of paper

Cellophane tape

Magic seeds will surprise everyone when they bloom in this window box.

TO READ

The Poetry of Flowers created by Keith Mosely

TO SING

Spring Flowers

Scale Song
Words by Anne Kaelin

I love all the flow-ers With col-ors so gay
That bloom in the spring-time And bright-en the day.
In gar-dens and mead-ows At this time of year
They bring us a mes-sage Of glad-ness and cheer.

ACTIVITY #31

CONCEPTS

Using your imagination

See if you can make your own paint, using only things you find in nature: dirt, berries, leaves, etc. Grind them down and add water. For fun, use a twig as a paintbrush. Soften the "brush" end by soaking it in water.

TO READ

The Blue Butterfly
by Bijou leTord

The gardens that Claude Monet planted were as much works of art as his paintings of them.

Illustrations by Sally Schaedler © Susan Striker

ACTIVITY #32A

TO READ

Redouté: The Man Who Painted Flowers
by
Carolyn Croll

CONCEPTS

Using your imagination

Texture

Sewing

Crafts

MATERIALS

Needlepoint canvas

Perle cotton thread

Needle

Masking tape

INSTRUCTIONS

1. To keep edges of needlepoint canvas from fraying, cut pieces of masking tape the width of canvas; place canvas edge on half of sticky side of tape and fold tape over onto other side.

2. Use a variety of stitches shown to create a lovely flower "painting" of your own.

Double cross-stitch   Cross-stitch   Bargello stitch

Eye stitch   Fern stitch   Chain stitch

64

Illustrations by Sally Schaedler © Susan Striker

Pierre-Joseph Redouté painted what he loved most—flowers. Paint a picture of your favorite thing.

CONCEPTS

Using your imagination

Painting with a sponge

Printing

MATERIALS

☐ White paper

🫙 Tempera paint

🖌 Brushes

🧽 Small pieces of sponges

INSTRUCTIONS

1. Using brushes, paint stems or vines on paper with various tints and shades of green or brown.

2. Dip sponges into paints and print on paper to create flowers.

ACTIVITY #32B

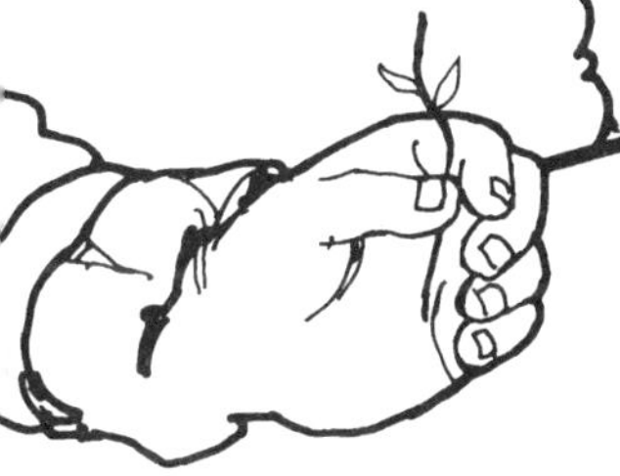

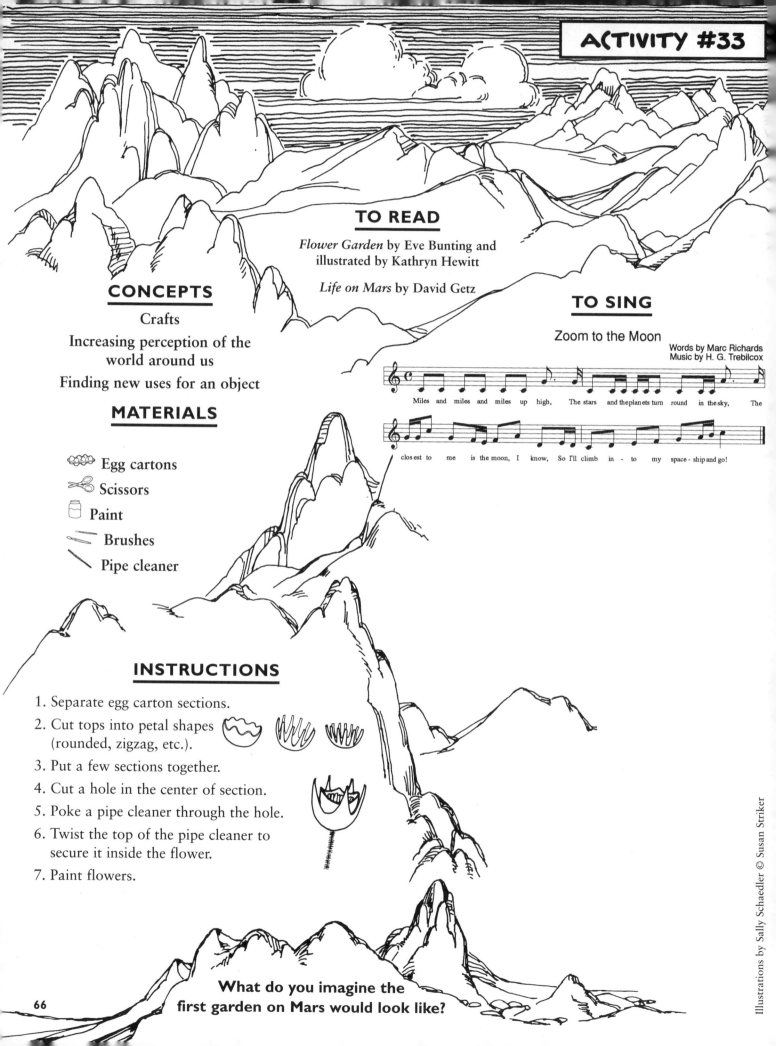

TO READ

Flower Garden by Eve Bunting and illustrated by Kathryn Hewitt

Life on Mars by David Getz

CONCEPTS

Crafts

Increasing perception of the world around us

Finding new uses for an object

TO SING

Zoom to the Moon

Words by Marc Richards
Music by H. G. Trebilcox

Miles and miles and miles up high, The stars and the planets turn round in the sky, The closest to me is the moon, I know, So I'll climb in-to my space-ship and go!

MATERIALS

- Egg cartons
- Scissors
- Paint
- Brushes
- Pipe cleaner

INSTRUCTIONS

1. Separate egg carton sections.
2. Cut tops into petal shapes (rounded, zigzag, etc.).
3. Put a few sections together.
4. Cut a hole in the center of section.
5. Poke a pipe cleaner through the hole.
6. Twist the top of the pipe cleaner to secure it inside the flower.
7. Paint flowers.

What do you imagine the first garden on Mars would look like?

66

Illustrations by Sally Schaedler © Susan Striker

CONCEPTS

Increasing self-awareness

Painting with a brush

Increasing perception of
the world around us

MATERIALS

Drawing paper

Pointed sable brush

Paint

Water

TO SING

Garden Song

by David Mallett

1.Inch by inch, row - by row, gonna make this gar - den grow;

All it takes is a rake and a hoe and a place of fer - tile ground.

Inch by inch, row - by row, some - one bless the seeds I sow;

Someone warm them from be - low 'till the rain comes tum-bl-ing down.

TO READ

Miss Rumphius by Barbara Cooney

INSTRUCTIONS

1. Paint flower stems.
2. Allow to dry.
3. Dip brush in paint; place down on paper.
   It will create the shape of a flower petal
   all by itself.

Illustrations by Sally Schaedler © Susan Striker

You must do something to make
the world more beautiful.
Start with your own backyard.

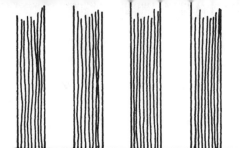

FLOWER

ACTIVITY #35A

CONCEPTS

Tints and shades

Color mixing

Pasting

MATERIALS

Colored tissue paper scraps

White glue diluted with water

Flowerpot

Brush

INSTRUCTIONS

1. Cut or tear tissue into small irregular pieces.
2. Paste all around flowerpot, overlapping colors to create new colors and values.
3. Cover completed flowerpot with a coat of white glue.
4. Allow to dry.

ACTIVITY #35B

To plant a chocolate kiss flower.

INSTRUCTIONS

1. Fold a small piece of cellophane tape with the sticky side out.
2. Connect two chocolate "kisses" at their bottoms to create a flower head.
3. Wrap with colored plastic wrap.
4. Secure with cellophane tape.
5. Begin to cover a wire stem with floral tape, inserting a paper leaf about halfway up. As you near the top, secure flower head on stem with tape.

MATERIALS

Cellophane tape

Chocolate "kiss" candies

Colored plastic wrap

Floral wire stems

Floral tape

Paper leaves

TO READ

Pearl's First Prize Plant
by A. Delaney

70

SHOW

On display is your prizewinning plant in a beautiful flowerpot.

1st

FOOD ACTIVITIES

CONCEPTS

Sewing

Cutting identical shapes

MATERIALS

Raffia

Yarn

Fabric scraps

White glue

Buttons or wiggly eyes

TO SING

The Farmer in the Dell

Old Singing Game

1. The farm-er in the dell, The farm-er in the dell, Heigh-ho, the der-ry-o, The farm-er in the dell.

2. The farmer takes a wife, the farmer takes a wife, Heigh-ho, the derry-o, the farmer takes a wife.

3. The wife takes a child . . .

4. The child takes a nurse . . .

5. The nurse takes a dog . . .

6. The dog takes a cat . . .

7. The cat takes a rat . . .

8. The rat takes a cheese . . .

9. The cheese stands alone . . .

INSTRUCTIONS

1. Cut two bunches of raffia for each scarecrow. Make sure the second bunch is twice the length of the first bunch.
2. Tie smaller piece at each end.
3. Wrap the second piece around the first and tie below "arms" and above "neck" to form head.
4. Separate raffia on the bottom to form legs and tie off at bottom of each "leg."
5. Cut out front and back of shirt at the same time. Repeat for pants or skirts.
6. Make clothes out of fabric scraps and sew fronts to backs.
7. Add details such as belts, shoes, or hats.
8. Decorate with buttons, wiggly eyes, sequins, yarn, etc.

Illustrations by Sally Schaedler © Susan Striker

TO READ

Feathertop: Based on the Tale by Nathaniel Hawthorne
by Robert San Souci

Barn Dance by Bill Martin, Jr., and Joan Archambault

Straw Sense by Rona Rupert and illustrated by Mike Dooling

Grandma's Garden by Elaine Moore, pictures by Dan Adreasen

The Little Scarecrow Boy by Margaret Wise Brown
and illustrated by David Diaz

**If you can build a scary enough scarecrow in the garden,
the birds won't come and eat the crops as they grow.**

ACTIVITY #37A

MATERIALS

- White paper
- Watercolor paint
- Water
- Vegetables and fruit
- Knife

TO READ

Play with Your Food by Joost Eiffers

Stone Soup by Marcia Brown

Frannie's Fruits by Leslie Kimmelman

Mean Soup by Betsy Everitt

Lunch by Denise Fleming

Green Eggs and Ham by Dr. Seuss

One Potato by Diana Pomeroy

Fruits: A Caribbean Counting Poem
by Valeria Bloom and
illustrated by David Axtell

CONCEPTS

Increasing perception of the
world around us

Relief printing

Pattern

INSTRUCTIONS

1. Choose a food from nature.
2. Slice it open, dip in paint, and print.
3. Repeat over and over on the paper to create a pattern.

ACTIVITY #37B

SILK FRUIT

CONCEPTS

Crafts

Sewing

Still life

Three-dimensional art

Making and using patterns

MATERIALS

- Silk fabric
- Textile paint
- Brushes
- Needle and thread
- Polyester fiberfill
- Scissors

INSTRUCTIONS

1. Make fruit shape out of paper. Trace it onto silk.
2. Hold two pieces of silk together, right sides facing in. Cut silk into the shape of fruit.
3. From wrong side, sew together leaving a small opening.
4. Stuff with fiberfill. Sew opening closed.
5. Paint with textile paints.

This cornucopia is overflowing with all your favorite foods.

INSECT ACTIVITIES

ACTIVITY #38

CONCEPTS

Pasting
Using your imagination
Increase perception of the
world around us

MATERIALS

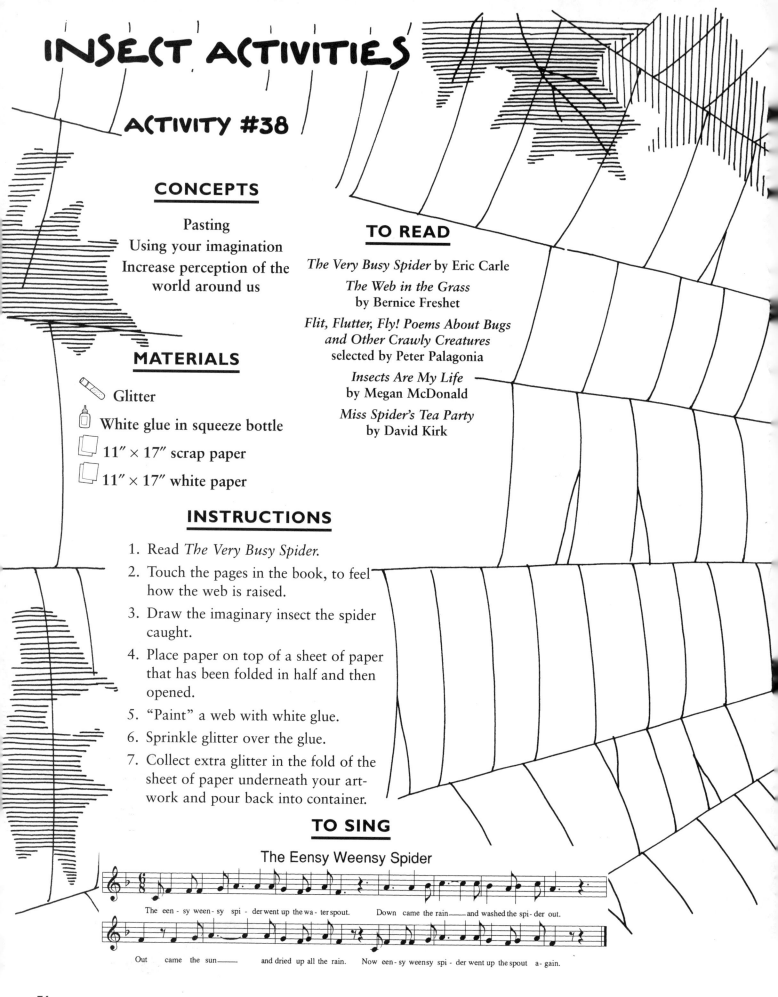

Glitter

White glue in squeeze bottle

11″ × 17″ scrap paper

11″ × 17″ white paper

TO READ

The Very Busy Spider by Eric Carle

The Web in the Grass
by Bernice Freshet

*Flit, Flutter, Fly! Poems About Bugs
and Other Crawly Creatures*
selected by Peter Palagonia

Insects Are My Life
by Megan McDonald

Miss Spider's Tea Party
by David Kirk

INSTRUCTIONS

1. Read *The Very Busy Spider*.
2. Touch the pages in the book, to feel how the web is raised.
3. Draw the imaginary insect the spider caught.
4. Place paper on top of a sheet of paper that has been folded in half and then opened.
5. "Paint" a web with white glue.
6. Sprinkle glitter over the glue.
7. Collect extra glitter in the fold of the sheet of paper underneath your artwork and pour back into container.

TO SING

The Eensy Weensy Spider

The een-sy ween-sy spi-der went up the wa-ter spout.   Down came the rain and washed the spi-der out.

Out came the sun and dried up all the rain.   Now een-sy weensy spi-der went up the spout a-gain.

**Sometimes spiders are surprised by
what they catch in their webs.**

CONCEPTS

Formal balance: Symmetry

Increasing perception of the world around us

Contrast: Light and dark

MATERIALS

- 15" × 18" white drawing paper
- Brushes*
- Black and two or more brightly colored tempera paints
- *Black and colored chalk can be substituted for paints

INSTRUCTIONS

1. Read the book *The Butterfly Hunt*. Study butterflies, noting symmetry and color contrast in their design.
2. Fold paper in half. Open.
3. With black tempera, paint one antenna on one side of the fold.
4. Fold paper and press. Open.
5. On one side of the fold, paint the top wing of a butterfly. Fold paper. Press. Open.
6. On one side of the fold, paint the bottom wing. Fold. Press. Open.
7. Still using black tempera, paint butterfly's body.
8. Allow black paint to dry.
9. Add color to the pattern on the wings. First apply paint to one side of the fold. Then fold. Press. Open.

TO SING

Butterfly

Words and music by Lynn Freeman Olson

Butterfly, but-ter-fly, where do you roam?

Whose luck-y gar-den do you call your home?

But-ter-fly, but-ter-fly, why won't you stay?

Why are you al-ways flut-ter-ing a-way?

CONCEPTS

Expressing emotions

Sewing

Cutting

TO READ

The Butterfly Hunt
by Ruth Wells

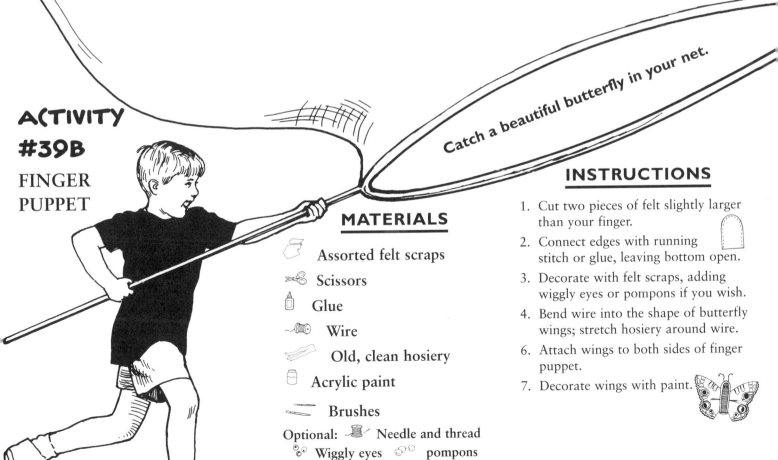

Catch a beautiful butterfly in your net.

ACTIVITY #39B
FINGER PUPPET

MATERIALS

- Assorted felt scraps
- Scissors
- Glue
- Wire
- Old, clean hosiery
- Acrylic paint
- Brushes

Optional: Needle and thread
Wiggly eyes   pompons

INSTRUCTIONS

1. Cut two pieces of felt slightly larger than your finger.

2. Connect edges with running stitch or glue, leaving bottom open.

3. Decorate with felt scraps, adding wiggly eyes or pompons if you wish.

4. Bend wire into the shape of butterfly wings; stretch hosiery around wire.

6. Attach wings to both sides of finger puppet.

7. Decorate wings with paint.

Illustrations by Sally Schaedler © Susan Striker

CONCEPTS

Utilizing geometric shapes

Increasing perception of the world around us

Pasting

INSTRUCTIONS

1. Read the book *Buzz Buzz Buzzing Bees* and observe how the bees build their honey combs by adding on hexagonal shapes.

2. Create your own beehive design by pasting hexagons on your paper in a unique design.

The Baby Bumble-bee

I'm bring-ing home a ba - by bum - ble bee:

Won't my mom - my be so pleased with me! I'm

bring-ing home a ba - by bum - ble bee:

Buzz, buzz, buzz, buzz! Whoops - it stung me!

MATERIALS

Paste

Background paper

TO READ

Buzz Buzz Buzzing Bees by Gene Fulks

TO SING

I'm squashing up a baby bumble bee:
Won't my mommy be so pleased with me!
I'm squashing up a baby bumble bee:
Buzz, buzz, buzz, buzz! Ooh—it's yucky!

I'm eating up a baby bumble bee:
Won't my mommy be so pleased with me!
I'm eating up a baby bumble bee:
Buzz, buzz, buzz, buzz! Ooh—my tummy!

LISTEN TO

"The Flight of the Bumble Bee" by Nikolay Rimsky-Korsakov

Illustrations by Sally Schaedler © Susan Striker

Help the bees build
their hive by adding
only hexagon shapes,
as they do.

CONCEPTS

Using your imagination
Architecture

MATERIALS

Assorted color markers

Paper

TO READ

Antics! by Cathi Hepworth

Two Bad Ants
by Chris Van Allsburg

INSTRUCTIONS

1. Read the book *Antics!* and look at the illustrations.
2. Discuss some of the needs of real ants.
3. If you were designing a utopia for real ants, where they would have everything they could ever want, what would it look like?

TO SING

The Ants Go Marching

1.The ants go march-ing one by one, Hur-rah, Hur-rah, - The ants go march-ing one by one, Hur-rah, Hur-rah, - The ants go march-ing one by one, The lit-tle one stops to suck his thumb and they all go march-ing down to the ground to get out of the rain, BOOM! BOOM! BOOM!

(continue similarly)
2. Two . . . tie his shoe
3. Three . . . climb a tree
4. Four . . . shut the door
5. Five . . . take a dive
6. Six . . . pick up sticks
7. Seven . . . pray to heaven
8. Eight . . . shut the gate
9. Nine . . . check the time
10. Ten . . . say "THE END."

Illustrations by Sally Schaedler © Susan Striker

82

These enterprising and hardworking ants are building an exciting new colony for their family of ten thousand ants.

Illustrations by Sally Schaedler © Susan Striker

A(TIVITY #42

CONCEPTS

Using soft drawing materials

MATERIALS

Fluorescent chalk

Facial tissue

TO READ

Ten Flashing Fireflies by Philemon Sturges

Fireflies by Julie Brinkloe

INSTRUCTIONS

1. Read one of the books listed.
2. Place a facial tissue under your hand to keep it clean while you draw. Draw fireflies onto the jar in your book with chalk.
3. If desired, smear chalk with a facial tissue.

TO SING

Come, Firefly

Hotaru Koi

Japanese Folk Song

Ho! Ho! "Ho - ta - ru koi" Bit-ter - wa - ter you will find
Ho! Ho! "Ho - ta - ru koi" At - chi no mi - zu wa

on that - side. Sweet wa - ter you will find on this - side.
ni ga - i zo. Kot - chi no mi - zu wa a - ma - i zo.

Ho! Ho! "Ho - ta - ru koi," Thro' the moun-tain road.
Ho! Ho! "Ho - ta - ru koi," Ya - ma mi - chi koi.

Come, come a - gain - with your lit - tle lan - tern bright.
An - do no hi - ka - ri de ma - ta ko - i, koi.

Spend a pretend summer
evening catching fireflies in this jar.

TREE ACTIVITIES

TO READ

The Ghost-Eye Tree
by Bill Martin, Jr.

Trees: a poem by Harry Behn

Sky Tree: Seeing Science Through Art
by Thomas Locker with
Candace Christiansen

CONCEPTS

Printing

Realism

Relief printing

Aesthetics

Increasing
perception
of the world
around us

ACTIVITY #43A

TO SING

I Am a Tree

by Madeleine A. Dufay

I am a tree on a very high hill, And most of the time I stand quite still,

But I'm not very still on a wind-y day, I swing and sway, swing and sway.

Tree Sanctuary

INSTRUCTIONS

1. Collect leaves.
2. Place one leaf on newsprint.
3. Roll brayer in tempera paint, then over leaf.
4. Move leaf to a clean sheet of newsprint.
5. Place white paper on leaf.
6. Press and smooth with your hands.
7. Repeat with other leaves until design is complete.

You can print with moss by dipping it in paint and patting it on a piece of paper. Flat stones, shells, and flowers can also be used to print.

To print a cattail, soak it in a jar of water, then apply paint with a brush. Roll or rub the cattail on your paper.

Experiment with making paint from nature. Crush the material and mix with water, oil, or egg yolk. Earth, plants, and animal products all provided materials for paints before the creation of modern paints.

MATERIALS

Leaves

Tempera paint in shallow pans

Brayer

White or manila paper

Newsprint paper

ACTIVITY #43B

Think of the roots of a tree as your toes in the sand, the trunk as a body, and the branches as arms and fingers reaching for the sky. If you were a tree, what would you look like?

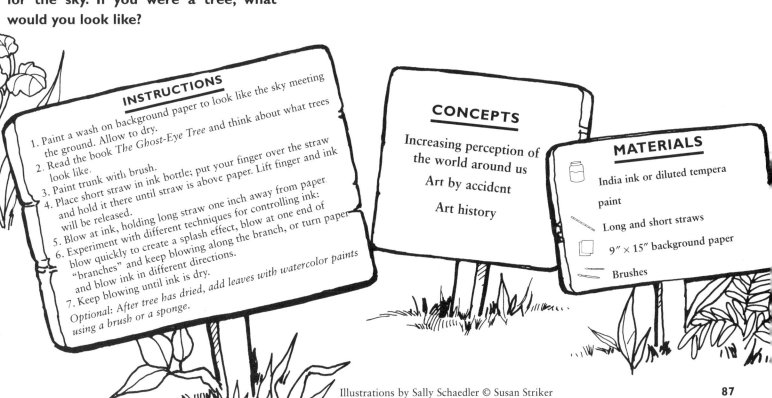

INSTRUCTIONS

1. Paint a wash on background paper to look like the sky meeting the ground. Allow to dry.
2. Read the book *The Ghost-Eye Tree* and think about what trees look like.
3. Paint trunk with brush.
4. Place short straw in ink bottle; put your finger over the straw and hold it there until straw is above paper. Lift finger and ink will be released.
5. Blow at ink, holding long straw one inch away from paper.
6. Experiment with different techniques for controlling ink: blow quickly to create a splash effect, blow at one end of "branches" and keep blowing along the branch, or turn paper and blow ink in different directions.
7. Keep blowing until ink is dry.

Optional: After tree has dried, add leaves with watercolor paints using a brush or a sponge.

CONCEPTS

Increasing perception of the world around us

Art by accident

Art history

MATERIALS

India ink or diluted tempera paint

Long and short straws

9" × 15" background paper

Brushes

ART CONCEPTS YOU WILL LEARN

I. Artistic Styles

Abstract art may be a distortion of what the artist sees in nature or it may consist simply of shapes, colors, forms, and textures that express an artist's idea of art.

Architecture is the art of designing buildings.

Art by accident occurs when an artist sets up the conditions that will produce the effect, but does not control the result. Materials react to each other or natural forces act on the materials.

Art criticism is the evaluation of a work of art to find its strengths or weaknesses and can be used to determine if constructive changes are possible or necessary.

Art history helps us to understand the past and our connections to other artists.

Craft objects are created with a function other than, or in addition to, the appreciation of their existence.

Cultural diversity. Art often contains the keys that have opened the secrets to the past for us. As we look at the art of a culture or period, we see reflected there the values and beliefs of that society.

Landscapes represent views of natural scenery.

Realism is the naturalistic representation of identifiable subject matter.

Still life is a drawing or painting of arrangements of inanimate objects like fruit, flowers, bottles, books, etc.

Surrealism is a twentieth-century art movement that attempted to represent in a realistic style the flow of unconscious thoughts that exist in the mind of the artist.

II. Color

Analogous colors are three colors situated next to each other on the color wheel.

Color mixing can be full of excitement and discovery. Colors can be changed and new ones created.

Complementary colors are two colors that are opposite each other on the color wheel and create the strongest contrast. When mixed together in equal amounts they create a neutral color. Red/green, orange/blue, and yellow/purple are the three sets of complementary colors.

Cool colors are on the blue side of the color wheel and are usually associated with water, foliage, and sky. Cool colors appear to recede when compared to warm colors.

Monochromatic color schemes are limited to tints and shades of one color.

Recognition and naming of colors is a skill that I believe is best taught one color at a time. Children learn that an almost infinite variety of tints and shades of one color can still be called by that color's name. Teaching more than one color at a time can cause confusion. Children through age seven will choose colors to use in their art for emotional reasons, which may appear "inaccurate" to adults but is normal and not to be discouraged.

Tints are colors that have white added to them.

Shades of colors have black added to them.

Warm colors are on the orange side of the color wheel and are associated with fire and the sun.

III. Design Principles

Background is the area of a composition that is in back of the dominant subject matter or design area.

Balance is a visual impression of equilibrium between the arrangements of color, form, shape, line, and texture in a work of art.

Center of interest is the part of a composition that first attracts the viewer's attention or interest.

Composition is the organization of the elements of a work of art.

Contrast is the polarity of the strong difference in things that appear together, such as light and dark, smooth and rough.

Esthetics is an intuitive, intellectual involvement or reaction to a form of beauty such as art or nature.

Foreground is the area that occupies the forward position of a composition and comprises the primary focus of interest.

Formal or symmetrical balance is a harmonious design created when identical shapes and colors appear on opposite sides of an imaginary center dividing line in a work of art.

Harmony is the visual "rightness" of a design or composition and gives a pleasing effect.

Horizon line is the line in a picture where earth and sky meet.

Informal or asymmetrical balance is a harmonious design with dissimilar-sized shapes and colors creating an overall sense of equilibrium.

Patterns are created by the orderly repetition of motifs on a surface. The word is also used to refer to adult-made forms for children to thoughtlessly duplicate. They should be avoided, as they stifle creativity.

Perspective is the art and science of representing three-dimensional objects on a two-dimensional surface.

Rhythm in art refers to the arrangement of art elements to achieve harmonious results. Rhythm can be created by continuous repetition, periodic repetition, or regular alternation of one or more of the elements.

Unity is the oneness or wholeness in the relationship between all of the elements in a work of art.

IV. Feelings and Personal Growth

Art career awareness can be an important aspect of studying art. There are many rewarding and secure positions in the arts. Often the starving artist is a cause of fascination and gets more attention than the hard-working artist who earns money, is productive, and is a respected member of society.

Art program publicity helps people understand that visual literacy is as important as verbal literacy and that sound art projects promote critical thinking and problem solving and encourage creativity and self-expression.

Expressing emotions through art activity is one important way of dealing with feelings and problems and can be therapeutic.

Group work in art is one way of learning to understand the value of participation and cooperation. At the ages of about nine and ten, children become aware of themselves as social beings. Community projects help them explore their place within groups, as each individual's contribution becomes important to the success of the group.

Increase perception of the world around us. Through observation and interpretation we learn through our senses, and heightening our sensitivity can be an important key to learning and creative thought.

Increase self-awareness. When we relate to an art experience and it is personalized for us, it can stimulate us into becoming more aware of our individuality and our relationships to other people and the world.

Using your imagination. The freedom to express imagination without risk is the essence of developing creative, insightful thinking. Albert Einstein once said, "Imagination is more important than knowledge."

Utilizing art to convey a message. From advertising to politics, art can be used to persuade and teach. We must remember that much of the information we have about ancient civilizations comes from analyzing the art they left behind.

V. Lettering and Symbols

Letters and numbers are used in art to emphasize a message or because of their intrinsic forms.

Symbolism is the representation of an object or the use of a color or shape to evoke a feeling or to send a message.

VI. Light and Shade

Contrast of light and dark is one of the many polarities that exists in nature. We can also contrast large with small shapes, curved with straight lines, etc.

Highlight is the area of a form that receives the most amount of direct light.

Shading is a darkened area that indicates the portion of a shape receiving less light than other portions of the form.

Silhouette shows the contours of an object filled in with a uniform color. The details of the object cannot be seen because the source of light is behind it.

VII. Lines

Line. A continuous mark.

Parallel lines exist side by side and are always the same distance apart.

Scribbling is derived from kinesthetic activity. Children spend from approximately age one through age five engaged in a process of exploring scribbled shapes and placement that can be identified when observed. Children should be encouraged to freely complete the scribbling stage by adults who show understanding and enthusiasm for this early art form. The lines and shapes contained in early scribbles form the foundation for all drawing and writing that comes later.

Rhoda Kellogg has observed and recorded children's scribbles:

1. *Dot*
2. *Single vertical line*
3. *Single horizontal line*
4. *Single diagonal line*
5. *Single curved line*
6. *Multiple vertical line*
7. *Multiple horizontal line*
8. *Multiple diagonal line*
9. *Multiple curved line*
10. *Roving open line*
11. *Roving enclosed line*
12. *Zigzag or wavy line*
13. *Single loop line*

Twenty Basic Scribbles		dot		multiple line overlaid circle		multiple vertical lines		roving enclosed line
		single vertical line		multiple line circumference circle		multiple horizontal lines		zigzag or wavy line
		single horizontal line		circular line, spread out		multiple diagonal lines		single loop line
		single diagonal line		single crossed line		multiple curved lines		multiple loop line
Adapted from "Analyzing Children's Art" by Rhoda Kellogg		single curved line		imperfect circle		roving open line		spiral line

14. *Multiple loop line*
15. *Spiral line*
16. *Multiple-line overlaid circle*
17. *Multiple-line circumference circle*
18. *Circular line, spread out*
19. *Single crossed circle*
20. *Imperfect circle*

VIII. Nature

Animals and plants share the world with us and help us understand our place in it.

IX. Proportions

Human Proportions. After emerging from the scribbling stage at approximately age five, the human form is usually the first thing children try to represent in their drawings. Teaching "rules" of proportion to children will serve to halt the important process of observation that leads to a deeper understanding of human characteristics and expressions.

X. Shape Exploration

Amorphic shapes are fluid and freeform and not related at all to geometry.

Concentric shapes are different-sized shapes on a plane with the same center.

Geometric shapes are regular forms such as circles, squares, triangles, octagons, etc.

Positive shapes in a composition are the objective shapes and forms in a composition, while **negative** spaces remain empty. In a good composition, positive and negative spaces should be of equal importance, and their relationship should be well balanced.

Using line to create shapes. Shapes are created when two points of a line meet.

XI. Shapes in Space

Armature is a framework like a skeleton that is inside a piece of sculpture and supports it, usually until it dries and hardens and can support itself.

Assemblage consists of three-dimensional objects attached to a flat surface background.

Clay coil method involves rolling long, thin, snakelike pieces of clay, which are used to wrap around the outer edges of a clay base and added, one on top of another, and sealed together to build up the sides of a bowl, pot, vase, or other container.

Mobiles are an art form invented by Alexander Calder, consisting of freely hanging forms in space that are carefully balanced in relation to each other.

Modeling with clay. Clay is an earthy material that is moldable when wet and hardens when exposed to high temperatures. Working with it provides children with an understanding of the three-dimensionality of shapes in space.

Optical illusions are created when patterns of two-dimensional lines, colors, and shapes give the impression of depth or appear to expand and pulsate.

Overlapping is extending one object over another. On a two-dimensional surface, overlapping can give the illusion that one object is farther away than the other.

Perspective represents the spatial relationships between three-dimensional objects on a two-dimensional surface.

Relief figures project from a background to which they are attached. Cut deeply, they are called *high relief*; cut out in a shallow fashion, they are called *low relief* or *bas-relief*. When sunken below the surface of the background, the term is *intaglio*.

Sculpture: Adding on. Three-dimensional design created by building up and attaching materials.

Sculpture: Removing. Three-dimensional design created by carving away from an existing form, such as a block of wood or stone.

Size relationships. Size is a relative concept. Comparative relationships between objects is what establishes their size. A large object can be said to be small when compared to a larger object.

Slip is liquid clay, used to attach pieces of clay.

XII. Technical Skills

Coloring in the outline of a drawing created by another person is not a creative activity. The only thing a child should color in is his or her own drawing.

Cooking and baking can offer opportunities to engage in creative activity.

Curling paper is done by putting a strip of paper over the sharp edge of a scissor and pulling the paper across it.

Cutting identical shapes can be done easily by cutting through several layers of paper or by **cutting on a folded piece of paper.**

Cutting paper requires sharp scissors. Often young children are given blunt scissors for safety, which is very frustrating. Safety can be taught early. The youngest child can learn to cut into paper and enjoy the empowerment of affecting the environment. Children should cut out their own shapes and should never be given adult-made shapes to cut out to learn cutting.

Developing photographs. Young children can understand the way chemical materials react to exposed light and can learn to develop black-and-white photographs.

Diorama is a scenic representation, usually in a box.

Drawing and painting on a fold can be a tool for teaching symmetry. A paper is folded, some paint or transferable drawing material is placed on one side of the fold, and one side is pressed against the other and rubbed; when the paper is unfolded, the design appears on both sides of the paper. A folded sheet of paper can also be used to produce a symmetrical picture when both sides are cut simultaneously around the fold.

Dry brush refers to a method of painting in which as little paint as possible is used so the brush stroke leaves paint only on some areas of the paper.

Dye is a fine soluble stain used to change the color of fabric or fiber.

Etching is an engraving process in which acid is used to eat lines into a metal plate. The design can be printed repeatedly on another surface. Safer variations of etching are more appropriate for young children, such as incised printing or crayon etching, which will not produce a printable surface. It does, however, form the foundation for understanding the more advanced technique.

Hard drawing materials, such as pencils, crayons, or markers, are good tools for precision line, cross-hatching, and coloring solid areas.

Impasto is thickly applied paint.

Incised process printing is done by using a sharp tool to etch the design below the surface of a printing block or plate.

Introduction to photography as an art form and to the principles behind the technical aspects of it is a basic skill in today's world.

Landscape is an outdoor scene of nature.

Lithography is an image drawn with a greasy medium on a smooth metal or stone block, covered with ink, and transferred to another surface.

Making and using patterns. One can learn that by making one's own original design and tracing around it, it can be repeated continually. Using adult-created patterns should always be discouraged and considered dishonest, in the same way cheating on a test is considered dishonest.

Making and using stencils. A stencil is a thin sheet of paper cut out so that designs can be produced repeatedly by rubbing paint or ink over and through the openings. As with any patterns, using adult-made patterns should be considered cheating.

Maps and diagrams are a synthesis of art and science, providing a visualization of abstract data, and can be endowed with artistic elegance.

Monoprint is a printing technique in which the design is created on a hard surface with inks and is reproduced only once by pressing it onto another surface.

Montage is a collage of photographs or parts of photographs.

Mosaic is a picture created by pasting colored stones, glass, or tiles to a flat surface.

Mural is a picture created for walls.

Mounting a picture on another, larger piece of paper to form a frame is an important aspect of presentation.

Painting with a brush provides many opportunities for producing varied effects. The side or tip of the brush provide different effects and different-sized brushes produce different lines, textures, and coloring.

Painting with a sponge. Dip sponges of assorted sizes and shapes in paint to use for painting or printing. This technique can produce interesting textures.

Painting with your fingers. Children learn kinesthetically and enjoy the tactile quality of the material. Direct contact with the paint and paper are important factors in this primitive form of expression. It can also be a satisfying way for a visually impaired person to be introduced to painting.

Paper-folding techniques require the manipulation of paper to create forms of both two and three dimensions.

Pasting is an everyday skill that can be frustrating because it is often self-taught. It is helpful for an adult to share tricks of pasting neatly, such as using a paste stick for applying the paste. This keeps the hands clean for arranging and placing paper, so that actual creative work can be the objective the child concentrates on. A picture that is pasted is called a **collage**, from the French word *colle* meaning paste.

Precision and measurement tools can be used to produce art as in science and math. These tools are used by draftsmen and architects and have their place in an art studio.

Portraits are pictures of people.

Printing is the process of duplicating multiples of a design by transferring it from the original surface or plate onto paper or fabric.

Puppets are small doll-like figures that can be moved by means of attached strings or by the hands.

Relief printing. On a printing block the surface to be printed is raised up. The block is inked, and the raised surface the only part of the block that touches the material to be printed on.

Rubbings are made by placing paper over a textured surface is and rubbing it with the side of a crayon or chalk to produce an impression of the original.

Sewing is attaching two pieces of fabric or other pliant material with needle and thread.

Scrafitto is produced by scratching lines into paint to reveal the original surface.

Sculpture is created by removing material from a block or by building up material, such as clay, to create a three-dimensional image.

Stabile is a stationary construction with moving parts.

Tearing paper creates a softer edge than cutting it does; it requires advanced manual coordination.

Tracing can be used as a tool for transferring a drawing from one sheet of paper to another, but tracing another person's art should *never* be used as a substitute for doing one's own original drawing.

Soft drawing materials such as charcoal, chalk, or oil pastels are perfect for blending colors, shading, and modeling forms.

Wax resist. Water resists the oil in wax and can produce interesting results.

Weaving is the ancient craft of intertwining threads, yarns, and other fibers.

UNDERSTANDING AND APPLYING MEDIA, TECHNIQUES, AND PROCESSES.

USING KNOWLEDGE OF STRUCTURES AND FUNCTIONS TO CONVEY IDEAS

CHOOSING AND EVALUATING A RANGE OF SUBJECT MATTER, SYMBOLS, AND IDEAS TO COMMUNICATE MEANING

UNDERSTANDING THE VISUAL ARTS IN RELATION TO HISTORY AND CULTURES

REFLECTING UPON AND ASSESSING THE CHARACTERISTICS AND MERITS OF YOUR OWN WORK AND THE WORK OF OTHERS

MAKING CONNECTIONS BETWEEN THE VISUAL ARTS AND OTHER DISCIPLINES